Thanks for your support

480/1000 Fr

Rod Cornelius

Ghetto Eyes

An urban anthology

Published by Akirim Press

© Copyright 2001
Rod Cornelius

This is a work of fiction. Names, characters, places, and incidents either are products of the author's imagination or are used fictitiously. Any resemblance to actual events or locales or persons, living or dead, is entirely coincidental.

All rights reserved, including the right of reproduction in whole or in part in any form.

ISBN 0-9708517-0-7
Library of Congress Control Number: 2001126593

Additional copies of this book are available by mail or website purchase order. Send $12.00 for each copy & 3.00 for shipping and handling to: Akirim Press, P.O. Box 30038, Columbia, SC 29230. Or contact us at www.akirimpress.com.

Printed in the U.S.A by

Morris Publishing

3212 East Highway 30

Kearney, NE 68847

1-800-650-7888

For my wife, Mirika

My parents, Tommie and Vera

My siblings;

Kevin, Mario, Mataya & Tom

Together, you are the force that moves me.

From the ship, thou see
a land of plenty.
Anchored, thou hope thine eyes be not covered,
For thou did not yearn this land discovered.
For free, thy wings shall spread,
And thy chirp shall add to all things said.

Colored Visions

December 2001

www.akirimpress.com

Acknowledgments

First and foremost, I'd like to thank my Lord and Savior, Jesus Christ. On so many occasions artists half-step when it comes to giving thanks to you. Jesus, I thank you for being my Savior and my everlasting role model. The life you led during your time on this earth is a precious blueprint of how I wish to guide mine on this planet. You, my Lord, I thank for everything you have given or taken away from me. I live for you and I love you.

I would like to thank my wife, Mirika A. Cornelius. Yes, my lady, the day has finally come and I owe a majority of my success due to your support. Since you've come into my life, you have raised every standard I've ever set for myself. Our success has just begun.

I'd like to also thank my parents Tommie & Vera Cornelius. If it weren't for you, there would be no me. If it weren't for you guys raising me and loving me the way you did, there wouldn't even be any words on this page. Thank you for everything Mom and Dad.

Shout Outs... Mario Cornelius, Jarod Anderson, Mammie Veal, George McFadden, Harvey & Dora Page, Willie & Louise Mayo, Darrel Mack, Abraham Meminger, James & Elaine Cornelius, Doris & Lee Bowen, Patricia & Anthony Scott, Janice & Charles Coleman, Lawrence Mayo, Hattie & Joe Wages, Haldon Sherwalker, John Swinton, Alberto Moore, Natalia Gleen, Greta Redmond, Sandra Suber, Tamece Dunson, Walter Hanclosky, Hope Isacc, Byron Weedon, James Bridgett, Willie Howell, Frank Myers, Myrna Izzard, Roydaros Wilson, Rodney Rhone, De'Eron Lee, Charless Savant, Edward "Boo" Johnson, Jackie Brown, Fatima Tillman, Eunice Perry, Tina Glover, Loletta Flowe, PFS, those SP Chicks, Bryan England, Gwen Kennedy, Michael Hatten, Ivan Cornelius, Angel Cornelius, Antonio Cornelius, Bryan Cornelius, Damon Stroman, Reginald Laroache (still wolfpack), Lamont Hollman, Stan & Carlotta Miller, Samuel Hartwell, Terell Bonnet, Latisha Hambrick, Akieta Douglas, BJ #71, James "Smitty" Smith, Ronnie Overton, Kim Jefferies, Kimico Wright, and anyone else I didn't mention. You know you weren't forgotten.

Contents

Welcome to the Ghetto...1
Love without words..2
The Answer..3
Loving U..4
Numbers...5
What's up with you..6
Elsie Mae...7
Did I?..8
Mr. Crack-head..9
Just Wondering...10
Prize in the Game..11
Game...12
On One Southern Day (slice of life)..................................13
Buxton's Day Off...32
Lord Have Mercy..33
Changes..35
Thoughtful Ties..36
Do You?..37
I Try..38
No, can I help you?..39
Yourself...39
I wish...40

Considerations...*41*
Waiting on Black Ivory..*42*
the man I am, the woman you are........................*43*
Mr. Policeman...*44*
The Best Kept Secrets (slice of life)......................*45*
Ghetto Eyes..*88*
Why am I here?..*89*
The Pimp, the Ho, the Consumer..........................*90*
One Day..*91*
Evolution..*92*
For Sale..*93*
Lil' Miss Shady..*94*
Banking on it..*94*
It was you...*96*
Indifferences..*96*
Sweet ole' Carolina..*97*
Ms. Mystery Woman..*98*
Is You?..*99*
Hated On..*100*
When it Comes Around (slice of life)....................*101*

Welcome to the Ghetto

Good Times, The Jefferson's and let's not forget Different Strokes--
Just a few of the scarce outlets for us po folks.
EBT cards, food stamps, and bey bey kids roaming the block,
And that big wooden fork and spoon in the kitchen hanging by the clock.
Welcome to the ghetto, where every month has a holiday on the fifteenth and the first,
And no one complains about missing a meal, 'cause things could be a whole lot worse.
Something like Junebug going too far and overdosing on some crack,
Or the police harassing and arresting you just because you're black,
Or getting an old fashion beat-down because the neighborhood bully thinks you're wack.
Welcome to the ghetto, a luxury in its own way.
Free cable, free food, and juicy gossip all in one day.
Black-eye peas, collard greens, pork chops, and don't dare forget fried chicken,
And that greedy relative coming unannounced wondering what y'all fixin'.
Welcome to the ghetto, no place like it in the world,
Where life seems so simple, but love is just as precious as a pearl.
And the good times may be overshadowed by the moments that make us sad,
But the meaning the ghetto gives to living certainly outweighs all the bad.

Love without words

Last night I had a dream and you were there--

Light brown eyes, caramel complexion, with your silky black hair.

You were sitting in the park licking on an ice cream cone

By the waterfall, on a bench, sitting all alone.

I waltzed to you-- nervous-- just like a kid on a first date,

Hoping that you'd stay right there; that I wouldn't run you away.

You sat there and smiled, sent chill bumps down my spine.

How I wished this wasn't a dream, and if it were, I wouldn't wake up this time.

But then I looked at you, and told you I loved you three times without moving my lips,

And it would really be something if you got up and blessed me with a kiss.

And it was like you understood every word I uttered through my simple stare;

That you knew whenever you needed some form of comfort, I would be the one there.

And then you got up, walked to me, and whispered words into my ear,

Told me that you loved me, grabbed my hands, on your face slid a tear.

The winds blew strong and a loud bell struck a sound that pierced throughout the lands.

Then I woke up, found myself covered in grass, straw and sand.

Dusted myself off, bowed my head, knowing again, I fell asleep a journey away from home.

And I took a deep breath, wiped my tears away, and wrapped my arms around your tombstone.

The Answer

I've been converged to consume
That in this world there is simply no room
To make any doubts before our tombs
That this world will be ending soon.
And in that, it's safe to say,
Through our breath, there's a greater pay,
And to redeem riches, there's another way.
Our purpose is to pray.
To see a pauper deprived of a dime,
To witness a worker earn nothing before his prime,
And to observe children perish before their time.
I think it's safe to say,
Through our breath, there's a greater pay,
And to redeem riches, there's another way,
Our purpose is to pray.
That alcoholic doesn't need another drink,
And that confused person shouldn't seek answers from that shrink,
And, oh goodness, scientists, it doesn't matter what you say or think!
It's really safe to say,
Through our breath, there's a greater pay,
And to redeem riches, there's another way,
Our purpose is to pray.

Loving U

Loving U is breathing the air I need to breathe,

The goal I need to succeed,

That comfort I so desperately need.

Loving U is a star falling out of the sky.

I think of it, I think of U, asking myself why?

Loving U is all that I have left.

I love U down to my final breath.

I'll love U forever and no one ever else.

Loving U is saying goodbye, right here and now.

Never seeing U again, that's what I must vow.

Loving U is loving U, the definition of my heart's pumping beat.

How just being in the same room with U makes sex so finite.

But I must go now as I think these words I speak.

Loving U are my days and my nights,

My wrongs and my rights,

My thoughts and my words,

My nouns and my verbs.

Loving U is leaving U,

And leaving U is loving U.

Numbers

Twenty, forty, sixty;
I got goals to meet and I need to meet 'em quickly,
But I can't supply the whole neighborhood when everyone's feeling so sickly.
Maybe it's time for my market to run out.
Maybe I should relocate before I lose all my investment in this drought.
All my customers, dropping like flies,
But there's all kinds of side-effects in this game, so this is no surprise.
So I guess I'll wait for a while before I make my final move.
Maybe I could start hitting up the little kids, then my sales would improve.
Might as well hook 'em while they're still small,
So their self-esteem won't be so high; they won't have so far to fall.
Look at me, always in that business state-of-mind.
And here comes Sarah, hope she brought some money with her this time.

Dime, twenty, dime, twenty;
Which one will he give me on credit, if any?
I need something to get me blasted off to somewhere like Mars.
I'm all out of money, but there's nothing wrong with what this girl does in the back of his car.
Shoot, at least I'm getting by,
And after I'm finished, I'll surely be catching me a high.
Oh, where did I leave little Rick?
Oh, he'll be alright; I need to hurry up and get this fix!

Todd will be home soon; he better wash them dishes and dump that trash can.
Hey, it's me Sarah! Come over here, Mr. Dope man!

Five forty-one, just about a quarter till six.
Momma left Ricky home alone in this cradle just to get her fix.
I thought she was gonna quit last week, but two days was her longest stint.
And I don't know when Grandma's gonna get fed up and stop paying our rent.
And yesterday was just awful 'cause I got suspended for fighting at school.
Scott said his brother paid Momma six dollars for a blow job in his pool.
God, I wish she would get some help before it's too late.
Aunt Georgia said she's gonna put it all to an end, and let us get taken by the state.
I don't want that to happen; I just want Momma to get some help.
I wonder if any of this would've happened if daddy hadn't of left?

What's up with you?

Yesterday, I met a man and thought he was black.
He looked black,
Talked black,
Even walked black.
I said, "What's up brother?"
He said, "Don't call me that!"

Elsie Mae

Somebody slapped the hell out of Elsie Mae!

Almost smacked her into the next day.

I don't really know what fo' but this here is what they say…

Elsie Mae, Elsie Mae,

No one in town likes Elsie Mae.

Screw your man if you got in her way.

Steal your money, make you broke all day.

But Elsie Mae went too far last Tuesday afternoon,

Slept all Monday night with Junebug, knew his wife was coming home soon.

And Rita, she been a full-figured lady.

Damn near everybody in her family get a check 'cause all them fools crazy.

But Rita 'pose to come back home Wednesday night 'round seven,

And there go Elsie Mae, nonchalant, laying up with Junebug, Tuesday, at a quarter till eleven.

Whole neighborhood outside relaxing on that hot summer day,

Then an overwhelming silence struck us all in the strangest way.

Huffin' and a puffin' up that dirt road hill,

It was Rita! That's when the whole neighborhood froze still.

She huffed and walked on.

We whispered, she walked on.

Huffed and puffed to that raggedy brown house.

"Why y'all so damn nosey? Can't a lady walk home without everybody all up in her mouth?"

She opened the door with that big, country smile shown,

While we all got ready, knowing Junebug wasn't alone.

She walked in, three second, "Elsie Mae, you stupid little bitch!"

We all burst into laughter as we listened to Rita's fit.

"Whap!" "Bang!" "Boom!" Them be the sounds from that shack.

Next thing we saw was Elsie Mae, thrown through the door, landing on her back.

"Elsie Mae, you low-down, no good, whore-being, trifling bitch.

If you ever come 'round here 'gain, I's put this foot right where I know now it'll fit!"

Elsie Mae, crying, got up and ran away.

Shamed by what happened, she knew there was nothing she could say.

Elsie Mae, Elsie Mae, somebody slapped the hell out of Elsie Mae--

Slapped her so hard, she had nothing else to say.

Did I?

Did I tell you, you are what makes my heart pump,
You're the answers to my questions when I'm stumped,
My savior when all my hope has sunk?

Did I tell you, you're the reason I know love,
The reason that I love, the root to all my love?
You are my definition of love.

Did I tell you, you are my sun, my heaven, my stars and moon,
Your love overflows me when it seems no more can be consumed?
Yes, you are my sun, my heaven, my stars and my moon,
But unmistakably, you are my universe.
Did I tell you that?

Mr. Crack-head

Hey, Mr. Crack-head,
No, I don't have three dollars you can borrow,
And I don't think I'll have it tomorrow.
No, I really don't need another VCR,
And I don't really wanna drive your car.
And, boy, you're beginning to look bad!
I heard you were an All-American football star; that's what I heard from my dad.
He said what happened to you is kinda sad,
But I shake my head and I kinda get mad.
For every three steps we go as a people, you bring us back ten.
And one day out of every week, you promise to stop, but here you come sucking on that pipe again.
So, no, Mr. Crack-head, I don't have three dollars you can borrow,
And I definitely won't have it tomorrow!

Just Wondering

Would things be different if I listened to my heart and convinced you to stay?
Would we be together if I ignored the fact that I had someone and took your hand anyway?
Would my life be better if I woke up every morning to your smiling grace?
Would I ever thirst, knowing that the sweetness of your wines would be all that I'd ever taste?
I don't know, but right now this life seems kind of homely,
Walking on this feeble planet, with a soul that's noticeably lonely.
Since you left, things just haven't been the same.
I often find myself daydreaming, scribbling out your name.
And I had the most beautiful dream not too long ago,
We made love by the sea, and I kissed you from your head to your toes.
Just one of my many fantasies since you left that dark, cold night.
Now I find myself contemplating, how close wrong really was to right?
Knowing that throughout life, you win just as many as you lose.
And it's hard as hell to sleep at night with a heart that's battered and bruised.
I don't know, but I was just wondering if you felt the same way too.
If so, I can be found where we last kissed, head down, eyes closed, reminiscing of you.

Prize in the Game

Now if you were as fine as you thought you were, you'd probably be blazed.
If you could get rid of that snobbish attitude, I'd honestly be amazed.
Just walking around, switching around, grinning like the world revolves around you,
Having unfortunates in your crew, not wanting anyone to outshine you.
With your tight jeans, tank-top and high heals a half size too small.
Don't want no honest-livin' brother 'cause sista' want it all!
You need a baller with a Lac sitting on some twen-twen-twenties.
And when that one gets locked up, you'd find another, since they're so dag on many.
All just to be a prize in the game,
And to have your name etched into the ghetto hall of fame.
But when it comes time for you to outlive all that ghetto-fabled drama,
You will have successfully graduated Deepintheghetto University as valedictorian of all baby mommas.

Game

Now roses are always red,

And I never saw a violet before, but I heard they were mostly blue.

And I don't want to approach you cliché, so I'll break you off with something new.

Now I'm no player, no pimp, no hustler, not even a big-time mack;

I'm just a Negro that likes what he sees, so, brown, are you diggin' that?

Girl, your light, almond eyes, sultry black hair and that pecan-brown complexion,

Gots me all wound up, straight checkin' myself for any sublime erections.

But, baby, I'm wide, wide awake, and you got my attention like a screaming captain.

Could I ask you just one question, right before you run off with your girls and start all that laughin'?

Would you bless me with your number? I know you're tired of hearing that,

But I'm a lonely, lonely man, remember, not a baller like them other cats.

I ain't got no game, no rhythm, no clout, not even a nice car.

My ideal of a classy date is lying on a blanket, staring at the stars.

And I know I'm not big-time, don't suspect I'll ever be.

No matter how hard I try, I can only be me.

So words may slip off my tongue as smooth as they wanna be,

But I can't help it, that's just me being me.

Now you knowing that, would you please be down with me?

And see if a brother with no game can take you where you wanna be...

On One Southern Day

She sat in the passenger seat passively gazing through the window of her SUV. She didn't need to drive today, besides, she's just about driven all the new out of it these past three weeks. No, today she'd let Maggie drive. They've been friends ever since Trish and her family moved down south. Maggie was the one to help familiarize her with southern living.

"Gosh, Trish, this thing rides so smoothly. No wonder you and Lester bought it," sneered Maggie as she handled the wheel as if it were made of fragile glass.

"It was Lester's idea, a treat to ourselves for getting the last of the leeches out of the house."

"Tom and I felt that same way when Liz went off to college. It was finally the freedom we waited so long for." Maggie slowly halted at a red light.

Trish looked out of her window and observed the scenery on the side of her when a sparkling, gold '78 Cutlass pulled beside them. A young black man was behind the wheel, wearing a baseball cap with a bandanna hanging from under it, and a mouth full of gold teeth. He looked over to her and winked his eye as his sound system trembled her truck. She nervously looked straight ahead as Maggie glanced to the side and frowned at the young man.

"Them and their loud music," she shook her head, "Where's a cop when you need one? All that racket he's making in this nice neighborhood!"

"It's alright Maggie. He's only a kid."

"Well, there are laws that state that garbage is a nuisance to our community."

"It is rather loud." She observed the guy pulling into the intersection.

"Of course it is!" Maggie crossed the street. "Could you imagine coming home and Will blasting that crap through your house?"

"Well, you know, Will has had his phase where he dabbed into that rap music, just not as loud though."

"Yeah, but Will's cultured. He's been raised to enjoy the finer things in life. You should be proud of that, Trish."

"Oh, you better believe I am."

"When that boy graduates from Princeton, he's gonna go somewhere."

Trish closed her eyes and smiled as she enjoyed the thought of her son's success. "How sweet it is, Maggie!"

"And it is sweet, Trish. Do you know the percentage of blacks that attend Princeton? Almost none! And for Will to get accepted, it's truly amazing. Tom and I were discussing it last night."

Trish smiled as she flipped the visor down and observed herself in the mirror attached to it. "Well, he worked hard enough for it, Maggie."

Trish's hair was silky black, with pecan brown eyes that matched her flawless complexion. At age fifty-three, her face was almost wrinkleless. On the other hand, her friend Maggie was just a few months older but her Caucasian skin did not contain the same youthfulness as Trish's did. Maggie's hair was gray like that of a squirrel's coat, and it was also thinning out at the top. Her face was consumed by wrinkles, almost making her look ten years older than she really was.

Maggie pulled into a parking space near the mall's entrance. "I really hope those young hoodlums aren't in there, infesting the mall again today. I can't bare being in an establishment where people just stand around, wasting time."

"I hear that. They need to go out and find a job or something."

Maggie turned off the car and looked at Trish. "Well, let's go shopping."

Trish observed her lips and licked them in front of the mirror. "Okay, I'm ready." She grabbed the latch and opened the door. They exited the car.

Maggie stood behind the truck and attempted to set the alarm with the key. "How in the world do you operate this do-hickey?"

"Here, let me show you," Trish grabbed the key and hit the alarm. The car made a brief honk to verify that it was locked.

"Technology these days!" Maggie stood amazed.

"Come on," Trish took the lead in heading towards the mall entrance. Maggie followed closely behind.

At the entrance stood a tall, white police officer. He kept his post as if he was guarding a heavily loaded safe. "How are you ladies today?"

"Fine," the ladies spoke simultaneously as they hurried into the mall.

"You just know when it gets close to the holiday season-- the security beefs up," Trish uttered out of the side of her mouth.

"And for good reason, too," sighed Maggie as she looked around and observed the hefty mall crowd. "Everyone wants something for nothing these days, and they want to evade the work to get it. Where's our nation heading?"

They entered the humongous department store, Lifestyles.

"I hope they still have sixty percent off on those dresses," Trish said as she gazed to the back of the store to the women's apparel section.

"I think I'll try to find myself one of those dresses also."

Trish rushed to a clothing rack and quickly picked through the clothing, searching feverously for her size.

Maggie slowly picked through the clothing opposite of Trish. "Plenty is still here. I guess we got here early."

Trish continued on her searching rampage, not replying to Maggie at all.

Maggie clutched her belly and looked around as her stomach rumbled. "Ooh, I have to find the restroom." She stared towards the back of the store and noticed the restroom entrance. "There, I'll be right back, Trish."

"Alright," replied Trish as she ceased at one colorful dress and observed it closely.

Maggie impatiently charged to her destination. Trish carefully inspected the size, price and length of the dress, all within a split second.

"You know, that dress isn't on sale," said a Caucasian saleswoman from behind her.

Trish, a little stunned, turned around with the dress in her hands. "What?"

"That dress, it isn't on sale," answered the woman as she grabbed the sleeve of the dress and gazed at the tag. "Someone must've placed it here on accident. Even the price is wrong on it."

"Then why are there others of the same style on this rack?"

The woman observed the clothing on the rack. "You're right!" She looked at the fifty percent sign on top of the rack. She sucked her teeth. "Oh, I see." She quickly snatched the sale sign off the top of the rack. "Someone placed this sign on the wrong rack!"

"Well that's not good."

"It sure isn't," said the lady as she stared at a young, black associate standing behind the counter a few racks down. "Doris!" she acquired the woman's attention.

The woman quickly approached them. "Yes, Ms. Hancock?"

"Did you place this sales sign on top of this rack?" she asked as she waived the sign in front of her face.

"Yes ma'am, I thought you told me to," replied Doris.

"Noooo, why would I tell you to place the sign on top of this rack when these items are new arrivals? Are our brains not working this afternoon? Hello?"

Doris frowned, "Well, it was mistake."

"Well, unfortunately, it was a costly one. Now we have to sale this item at a severe discount because you can't seem to follow directions."

"No, I'm not interested in purchasing the dress. I was just looking at it," Trish said modestly.

"No ma'am, Lifestyles is committed to one hundred and ten percent customer satisfaction," Ms. Hancock solidly announced.

"Ma'am, I apologize for the mistake," Doris sincerely pleaded.

Ms. Hancock rolled her eyes.

"It's fine," replied Maggie. "No harm at all. Everybody makes mistakes."

"Ma'am, on behalf of Lifestyles Inc., I would like to apologize for our ex-associate's blunder and we..."

"Ex!" snapped Doris.

"Just one moment please," replied Ms. Hancock as she raised her finger in front of Doris' face.

"Hell no!" screamed Doris as she swiped the woman's finger out of her face. "I told the lady I was sorry and you're just gonna fire me over some damn mistake that you actually made?"

Trish grinned.

"Look, I will discuss this matter with you in the proper area. This is not the time nor the place."

"You already done fired me, so I think this is the proper area," yelled Doris.

"Doris, just calm down before you do something foolish. I don't want to be forced to call security."

"Oh, kiss my ass, bitch!" Doris snatched off her name tag, threw it on the floor, and stormed out of the store.

Ms. Hancock's mouth dropped. "I can't believe she just behaved that way."

"My word," said Trish, "It really wasn't that much of a problem. I wasn't even set on purchasing the darn thing."

"Oh, I'm sorry, but I have got to promo this dress for you right now.

Never should a customer be exposed to the type of behavior that you've just witnessed. I just don't understand what got into her."

"Some people just don't know how to handle anger, I guess," smiled Trish.

"That is no excuse to display such putrid behavior in front of a customer. Ma'am, I'll be right back." Ms. Hancock rushed to a register with the dress in her hand.

Trish turned around and began looking on another rack. Maggie approached her.

"I feel much better now. I don't like using public restrooms, but that time, I had to make an exception," said Maggie as she rubbed her belly. "You found anything yet?"

Trish walked closely to Maggie and began to whisper out of the side of her mouth. "Let me tell you what just happened over here. Why did I just get a free dress because one of those hot-headed sales associates just had it out with their superior?"

"You've got to be kidding me."

"Do you know she told her boss to kiss her you know what, right in front of me?"

"No," replied Maggie.

"Now there are certain things that you just don't do."

"I'm not kidding."

"Oh well, I gained a dress, and she lost a job."

"People just don't seem to care anymore," said Maggie as she searched through the rack. "Oh, I like this." She pulled a shirt off of the rack.

"Now that is nice, Maggie. I'd bet that would look good on you, too."

Maggie placed the shirt on top of her breast and stretched the sleeve out to her arm's length. "You think Tom would like it?"

"Of course he'd like it. It's a knock out. Go try it on."

"I don't know." She pulled it down and glanced at the tag. "Fifty-three dollars is a lot of money for just a top. Tom would have a hissy fit."

"Now why do you think Tom's working in the first place?"

She blushed. "So I can spend!"

Ms. Hancock approached the ladies with a bag in her hand. "Here you go, ma'am." She handed Trish the sack. "I truly apologize for the inconvenience."

"Trust me, it's alright," replied Trish. "Hey, where's your fitting room? She wants to try something on."

"It's right here," said the woman as she pointed at the room directly behind them.

"Thank you!" Maggie took the dress off it's hanger and slid her purse off of her arm. She briefly glanced at Trish.

"I'll take...," mumbled Trish with her hand out.

Maggie quickly turned to Ms. Hancock. "Could you hold my purse for me while I'm in there?"

Trish stood puzzled.

"Sure, ma'am," the woman grabbed the purse.

"Well, I'll be back Trish," Maggie entered the fitting room.

Baffled, Trish walked across the aisle into the men's apparel section. "Did I bring my..." She said to herself as she opened her purse and began digging through her credit cards. Suddenly, a gentleman bumped into her and dropped his pager. All of her cards spilled onto the floor.

"Oh, my bad," said the man as he picked up the cards. "You okay?"

"Yes, I'm fine," she replied.

He handed her the credit cards and bent over to grab his pager off of the floor. Trish suddenly realized that the gentleman was the same young man she saw in her car earlier.

"Hey, you're..." She pointed at the man.

The man smiled allowing his gold-laced teeth to shine brightly.

"What? You know me?"

"No, not really. I just remembered seeing you in my car earlier."

"Really?" He blushed. "You're a little ripe for the kind of style I kick, aren't you?"

She lightly nodded her head. "Not a big hip hop fan at all."

He observed his pager and noticed it's clip was broken. "You know, that's cool. That's cool. You probably listen to something a little more vintage, right, like some Four Tops or The Temptations, something like that, right?"

She frowned and shook her head, "More like Beethoven and Mozart."

His head snapped up, "For real? I didn't think black folks listened to that kind of crap. You must be got some money or something, right?"

She frowned, "My husband and I are very well established."

"Husband!" He jokingly looked around. "I don't wanna make my man mad at me! I'm not trying to pull nobody's woman."

She rolled her eyes. "My husband is not a jealous man. Besides, he's at work right now. I'm here with a friend."

"That's cool." He tried to re-attach the clip on his pager.

She carefully studied his struggle with the minute contraption. "Are you a drug dealer?"

He paused and slowly looked up. "What?"

"Well, I know you can't be a doctor."

"Why every brotha' with a pager gotta be a drug dealer?"

"Well, you know what the news illustrates."

"Damn! You mean to tell me that you've been around white folks for so long that the only way you know about your own people is through the news?"

"That's not true," she rebelled.

"That's how it sounds to me!" He shook his head. "You sound just like most of those white folks, anyway! 'Every black man is slangin' drugs or doing something wrong'. Shit! When the fuck are you gonna wake up? I don't have to do nothin' illegal. I work damn near fifty hours a week, in the hot ass sun, diggin' ditches for your information!"

Trish was slightly embarrassed as the man walked away. "Hey, I'm sorry! I didn't mean..."

"Ah, go look in the mirror, you Uncle Tom!" The man stuffed his pager in his pocket and stomped out of the store.

Ashamed, she looked around to see if anyone was paying any attention to the incident. No one was around. She walked around to the fitting room as Maggie walked out with the blouse in her hand.

"Trish, this top is perfect," smiled Maggie.

Trish quickly faked a smile to hide her uncomfort. "Is it?"

"Yeah, but..."

"What is it?"

"Well, Trish, you know I hate asking for favors but..."

"What is it Maggie?"

"I sort of don't have fifty-five dollars on me right now."

"Oh please, I got it!"

"You know, I'm all out of checks. Just drop me off at the bank after we leave here and I'll get it right back to you."

Trish opened her purse. "Don't even worry about it, I'll just charge it on my platinum card."

They walked to the counter where Ms. Hancock stood. She bent over and handed Maggie her purse.

"Here you are, ma'am," said Ms. Hancock. "Did you find everything okay?"

Maggie grabbed the purse. "I must say I did."

Trish fondled through her purse but appeared to have a little trouble finding what she was searching for.

Maggie stared at Trish as Ms. Hancock took the dress and scanned it's tag. "Do you have everything, Trish?"

A little frustrated, "Well, I can't seem to find my platinum card."

"Did you bring it with you?"

"Of course. I had it when I was over…." She froze as her eyes almost popped out of her head.

"Trish, what is it?"

"Ma'am, is everything alright?" questioned Ms. Hancock.

She looked towards the aisle where she stood earlier. "I had it just before that guy bumped into me."

"Oh my God, you've been pick-pocketed!" yelled Maggie.

"I…," muttered Trish as her hands began to tremble.

"Ma'am, I'll call mall security, right now." Ms. Hancock quickly picked up the phone behind the counter and started dialing.

"Trish, do you remember who the guy was?"

"Yeah, it was the young man in that gold car from earlier today."

"I remember him," said Maggie as she looked towards the exit. "I bet he's still in here somewhere, too."

"He just left here."

"Come on, there's an officer standing right by the main entrance. We can probably stop him before he makes it out of the parking lot!"

The two women rushed out of the store. They hurried through the mall into the food court, looking left to right simultaneously.

Maggie looked towards the main entrance. "Trish, isn't that him?"

She carefully observed the man as they quickly stomped towards the exit behind him.

"I don't know," cried Trish.

The man exited the mall as they ran towards the doors.

"I think, I think...," Trish uttered, still unsure.

They walked out of the mall and froze on the sidewalk beside the officer.

"Yeah, it's him! It's him!" screamed Trish.

The young man continued on his way down the row of cars.

Maggie quickly turned to the cop. "Officer, that man just pick-pocketed my friend!"

"What?" yelled the officer as he stared down the row of cars.

"That man, he just stole my friend's credit card!" yelled Maggie.

The officer left his post and began to jog down the row of cars and approached the young man. "Excuse me sir! Sir!

The women stood back and closely observed.

"He'll take care of that thief," smiled Maggie.

The young man stopped at his car and turned around. "What the hell did I do now? Y'all don't get tired of harassing people?"

The officer slowly approached the man. "Sir, I need you to step away from the vehicle?"

"Hell no!" yelled the man. "I ain't do nothing."

The women looked on as a few mall visitors stood behind them.

"It looks like he's trying to resist the officer," said Maggie.

"Sir, I'm not gonna ask you again; step away from the vehicle, please," said the officer.

"Tell me what for?" questioned the man.

The officer grabbed the radio by his side. "Officer Murk requesting back up on the east main entrance."

"Man, tell me what you want."

The officer re-attached the radio to his waist. "I just wanna ask you a few questions. So come along before every thing gets a lot worse than it already is."

"No!" said the young man as his pager sounded off. He quickly dug into his pocket.

"Don't move!" The officer quickly grabbed for the gun on his waist.

The young man's eyes bulged open as he pulled his pager out of his pocket. The officer released fire on the man. He fell to the ground as his pager cracked on the asphalt beside him.

Maggie and Trish's mouths widened as they watched.

Hours Later

Trish silently drove her truck down the streets of a residential area. Maggie observed her every move.

"You know, it wasn't your fault," said Maggie.

Trish's eyes stayed glued to the trek of road before her as she ignored Maggie's comments.

"They found ten pounds of marijuana in his car, Trish!" She shook her head. "He was a drug dealer!"

A tear slid down Trish's face. "They didn't find the card on him."

"He probably threw it away before the officer got to him. They work quick, Trish."

"I killed him, Maggie. A boy died because I accused him of something he didn't do."

"Trish, you're talking nonsense."

She stared at Maggie. "Am I?"

There's a long pause between the two as Maggie gapes at Trish, trying to think of something to say.

"Trish, you didn't kill him," Maggie blushed. "They found drugs in his car. You did our community a favor. That bugga-boo got what he deserved!"

Trish quickly slammed on brakes. "What in the hell did you say?"

"What?" Maggie defensively replied. "You did this community a favor?"

"No, after that!"

"What? That bugga-boo got what he deserved! He did Trish."

Trish frowned. "What in the hell do you mean by bugga-boo?"

Maggie childishly giggled. "Oh, come on Trish. I know you're not taking offense to that. You're just angry. It'll be alright."

"Maggie, where in the hell do you get off calling someone a bugga-boo?"

"Come on, Trish, it's not like I called him a nigger or something. Even though that's what he was."

Trish frantically shook her head. "Where in the hell is this coming from?"

"Trish I know you're not taking offense to the word nigger. I mean, you know you're not one. Tom and I never considered you nor anyone in your family as one. And we both know those who qualify under that description and you are far from being any inkling in that category."

Trish closed her eyes and took a deep breath. "Maggie, you have less than three seconds to get the hell out of my car."

"Trish! Why are you acting like this?"

"Get the hell out of my car!"

"Trish!" she uttered as she grabbed the latch and cracked the door open.

"Get out!" she shoved Maggie out of the car. Maggie tumbled onto the street as Trish slammed her door shut and sped off.

"Trish!" yelled Maggie as she jumped off of the pavement. "Trish! What are you doing?"

Trish swiftly zoomed down the street with tears fluttering down her face. She approached her house and drove recklessly across the lawn. She parked the car, grabbed her purse and exited the vehicle. She raced to her porch, unlocked the front door and ran into the house without closing the door. She ran into the bathroom and emptied her purse into the sink.

She searched through all of the contents in the sink, throwing items on the floor once she picked them up. She threw makeup, pills, papers and pictures all on the floor in search of one specific item. She froze suddenly. Her hands trembled as she put the card before her soiled face. It was the platinum card she accused the young man of stealing.

She tightly shut her eyes and ripped the piece of plastic in half. She opened her eyes and stared at the reflection in the mirror before her. All she could do was shake her head, knowing that her accusations cost a man his life. She balled both her fists and pounded on the mirror. It shattered leaving her hands bloodied. She stared at the outside of her severed hands and sat on the edge of the tub behind her as she dropped her head and cried.

The End

Buxton's Day Off

Buxton had been working six months straight.

He barely slept, saw his kids, or went on any dates.

Buxton became a bonafide, certified workaholic!

Straying far from his pops and two uncles, five-star alcoholics!

But Buxton buried himself in his work;

Sleeping in his clothes, pants, shoes, and shirt.

Managing the king of fast-food, Burger Palace.

Folks say he became so indulged with working because of his break up with Alice.

Nevertheless, he was at work from five in the morning till eleven at night.

Until one morning he woke up and thought that something wasn't right.

He thought about his kids, his son Tim and daughter Elaina,

How his baby-momma was doing, even though she was a constant complainer.

He thought about Alice, how he caught her in bed with another dude,

And how that experience affected him-- to every lady he met he was rude.

He thought about how Burger Palace had became his life and took him away from his world.

How he sunk from his loved ones, just because of a girl.

And to make things worse, she wasn't even all that.

So Buxton jumped out of bed and yelled, "I want my life back!"

"Never should I avoid seeing my kids, letting them think I'm out of the mix. And what's up with my baby-momma? I still love her, although she always bitch, bitch, bitch!

And forget Alice-- that's what I get for picking up hoochies at the strip clubs.
She probably would've left up out of there with any nigga flashing a few dubs.
I'm getting up out of here and I'm gonna chill today.
Ain't gonna let no depression send me to an early grave this way!"
So Buxton did it, got out of bed and jumped in the shower.
The boy was smelling kind of bad, so he bathed for about an hour.
He drove to his baby-momma house and took the kids out for the day.
He even let his baby-momma come along even though she complained most of the way.

Lord Have Mercy

Lord have mercy on me for I've sinned a lot in this life.
I've done a lot of sinning, and spoke a lot of words that weren't very nice.
I've had dirty thoughts at the strip clubs, and attended during the week more than twice.
Lord have mercy on my soul because I can lie with a straight face,
Fornicate, steal, and tell all my lies in the same place.
Lord, have mercy on me because I wanna change my ways,
And I wanna go along with you, Lord, before the end comes to these final days.

The Last Time

You said it would be the last time his name would ever be announced,
That I would never hear anything about him in this house,
That this future was for you and I together.
It was the good and the bad from then on, that's what we had to weather.
You asked a lot of me when you begged me to once more trust you.
I exercised so many changes to my world, just because of you.
Now I see his name again,
I speak this name again,
Some brothers just can't get a win.

You said you didn't want me talking to her anymore.
All your friends told you she wanted me and she wasn't nothing but a whore.
YOU believed she had her eyes on me even though she never made a pass.
So I ended that relationship even though I never touched her ass.
And I did that for our sake.
But some brothers just don't get a break.

So you tell me I'm wrong,
And I'm the one breaking up this happy home,
That I need to chill and accept the cards being dealt.
But I don't think you understand my feelings and what it is that's being felt.
So, no, I'm not the one breaking up this happy home,
And you actually don't have to leave that nigga alone,
But when you turn around one day, don't wonder why this brother's gone.

Changes

Strip clubs, fast chicks, and bottles of Moet,
Dime bags, Philly blunts, and hot, wet sex.
My eyes love and lust.
On that young dime, I'm 'bout to bust.
I love this world the Lord has given us.
No, I'm not ready to change yet.

Sunday morning church, that preacher seems to be talking to me.
Could he possibly know all those things are describing the life that I lead?
That I curse, fornicate, and smoke the finest of weed?
And I have a good girl, but I still do things that qualify me as a candidate for HIV?
Pump, pump, pump; my heart goes beat!
I'm ready to change now.

Girl looks at me like she wants to rip my clothes off.
Took her inside the restroom, she ripped my clothes off.
She went downtown on me; it felt stupendous.
Next time I'll bring some friends; she'll do every last one of us.
I'll say I spent the night at Mike's, got no time to hear that fuss.
You know I ain't ready to change.

That cop has a gun to my head.
One false move and I could end up dead.

He should be out fighting crime, but he wants to harass brothers instead.
If I make it out of this one, I'm praying to God right before I go to bed;
Ask Him for forgiveness because this world is just too much.
Ask Him to give His love to me with His everlasting touch.
Yes, I'm ready to change.

Just one more time, I know He wouldn't mind.
Ooh, she looks so damn good, that skirt revealing all of her behind.
Just her and I tonight, no one gotta know,
I'll even go to church tomorrow and give the pastor what I owe.
And maybe that should make up for what I'm about to do with this ho.
Cough, cough, cough; I can't breath anymore.
And what's this? I can't move; I'm lying here on this floor.
SORRY CHILD, IT'S TOO LATE FOR YOU TO CHANGE!

Thoughtful Ties

I thought I was in love with you-- yes I did!
I thought we'd get married, buy a house, have some kids.
I thought we'd live together, forever, understanding the purpose of our endeavor.
I'd never leave your side, and I did mean never.
I thought he was just a friend, kind of like Jack and Jill.
But too much thinking lacks awareness and that part of thinking is unreal.

Do You?

Do you know how stupid you look, talkin' 'bout you a baller?

Braggin' 'bout having a good girl, but never callin' her;

Got the nerve to say pimpin' ain't easy,

But I ain't never seen a pimp with elbows that ashy and a head that peasy.

Do you realize common sense just ain't that common?

But I realized you didn't when you said you were going out robbin',

Stealin' and knockin' down your own kind!

Boy you couldn't be no child of mine.

It would take the force of the Lord to keep my foot out of your behind.

Do you realize how silly you look with them gold fronts, talkin' 'bout you got bank!

But them fronts only tell me your teeth are rotten and your breath is stank!

In about fifteen years they'll probably all fall out.

And being you never went to school, you won't get'em fixed 'cause you won't have no clout.

I Try

I try to forget the way you smell,

The way my heart thumped when I fell,

How I knew it was love, yet I tried so hard to rebel.

I try to forget how soft your body felt when we hugged,

How I screamed your name out when we made love,

How I woke up the next morning and you were all I thought of.

I try to put my memories of you in the back of my mind,

Make this thing we had finalized,

But I still love you is what I realize.

Yet, I try and try again,

Putting on charades for all my friends.

The feelings I have for you just won't end.

And I try not to believe I love you,

That this life I live will be just fine without you,

But if this is not true, then I guess I'll never be set free,

Because in this lifetime there can never be any you and me.

No, can I help you?

No, can I help you?

You seem to be the one looking for something.

Acting like I come in this store to steal something.

Why it gotta be 'all black folks steal'?

When y'all good folks been stealing since the invention of the wheel.

And you following me, like you're such a good citizen.

What about all this land you and your good folks stole from those Indians?

You good folks just murdered that entire race,

And you come following me like I'm out of place?

Look at you, not a darn thing to say.

Who do you think built this country your store is in anyway?

Not your lazy ass ancestors, them souls burning in hell right this minute.

So back off, get out of my face, I'll let you know when I'm finished.

Can you help me? Hell no, you can't help me!

Just go on behind that counter, think about what your ancestors done, and stop sweatin' me.

Yourself

Always self, and no one else,

Your depiction on the way life should be.

I give you the world and all but anything's returned to me.

I wait the table you eat,

Make the bed you sleep,

Clean the shoes you wear,

And tidy the home you stare.

I flow the way you flow.

I know myself no more.

Why is it so hard for you to think of someone else besides you,

To love someone else besides you,

To think someone else deserves affection besides you?

Hmmm, for it won't be long before reality strikes your eyes,

That something about my presence will come to your surprise.

All my affection, love, and happiness you chose to ignore

Won't even be an issue because I won't be here anymore.

I Wish

I wish I didn't give away my first kiss.

All it's innocence and purity,

It's ignorance complimenting it's beauty.

Patience was a useless endeavor,

For just a few miles down the road, my destination awaited.

I wish I never slid inside,

For confidence overshadowed my inexperience,

And my home outside my burrow led me to believe
A man's journey begins when he sails his first sea,
But it is I who I am not, a nomad, but a squatter,
And it is that first brick that initiates the foundation.

I wish I didn't give my heart to her.
Strained is my trust and suspension of disbelief,
For once scarred, my wound never healed in total capacity,
And if the horrors of reality had never been seen,
My reality to fall in love would not be just that-- a wish.

Considerations

I don't expect you to know how it feels to be me,
To see me for me, not a color, but me for me.
I don't expect you to know how it feels to be watched, whispered about, and harassed when I go shopping.
Or how it feels to be driving in front of the police-- terrified about turning or stopping.
I don't even expect you to have sympathy for me when you hang that flag on your house, truck or state capital.
I guess all your feelings are just that habitual.
But it would be nice if you knew that sometimes your flag offends me;
That the people that created that symbol enslaved my people and were their enemies.

It would be nice if you knew that I don't eat at certain barbecue outlets since they never intended on serving folks with the color of my skin.

In the early days, in those same restaurants we had to order from the back, The owner didn't want us to come in!

It would be nice if you knew that even though your people did a lot of dirt in the past, it never stopped, just performed in cunning new ways.

But it's nice to know there will be reparations as we approach the final days.

Waiting on Black Ivory

Sunny days, charcoal nights,

My mind wanders on your whereabouts.

Where is that dark, brown ivory that slowed my speedy world down?

That dark-colored girl, with them juicy fruit lips,

Nice, slender bones with them "nigga I know ya' following me hips!"

Black ivory, in my heart you bring that tickle,

Got those old ladies asking, "What in the world is he doing with that pickle?"

But me, I'm never the one for veggies or fruits,

And that produce in my pants is not produce in my pants,

You know damn well I wanna knock them boots!

So back off old bitties, this mind is salivating,

Sweet love, I'm contemplating,

With all these un-erected flows, I'm incubating.

On you black ivory, I'm waiting.

Yes, black ivory, I am waiting.

the man I am, the woman you are

it feels like yesterday, the first day I ever met you.

had a woman, by no means I should've sweated you!

but I did, opened like the rim on a jar.

our conversation flowed like the motion to a car,

but every word you uttered went through one ear and out the other.

for my eyes followed your physique and kept my mind in the gutter.

by no means I wanted a one night stand,

maybe a few dates, the motel room, and the role of that part-time man.

but things went further, and by far, out of my reach.

no matter how much I alluded you, you clanged to me like a leech.

the irony is-- my ego let you continue to suck me in,

and an argument with my lady would just be an excuse to let you in.

then things got complicated; you told me you had begun to harvest my seed.

just another ounce of drama, and one more thing my life did not need.

you expressed your sincerity when you realized the harvest was hurting me,

so you terminated your crop, but vowed leaving me would not be as easy.

for it was I, the reason that evacuated every moral that resided in your temple.

and it was my presence and dominance that made your sinning so simple,

I was the cancer in your life that was slowly killing your soul,

and our love affair had gotten too far out of control.

NO, my intentions were never for your own good,

But if your heart can't tell you wrong from right, then who in the hell should?

Mr. Policeman

Mr. Policeman, did I really deserve to get a lecture about how bad us niggers are,
How my ride resembles that drug dealer's car,
How I try to dress and act like I'm a rap star?

Mr. Policeman, do us people really make you sick?
Do we really steal from hard-working white folks that quick?
Are you really that tired of all my bullshit?

Mr. Policeman, did you really have to put those cuffs on me that tight?
Do I really look like the type of brotha' goes looking for a fight?
Did you really have to shine that light in my face that bright?
Did you really have to hit me in my stomach that hard last night?

Mr. Policeman, how did it feel to severe my health,
To punch me so hard, it took me fifty seconds to capture my breath.
That you were stuck with nothing else--
For you to do such things I know not to call the police for help.

The Best Kept Secrets

𝒯hroughout life, you go through many different situations. Some go much more in depth than others, but with each obstacle one comes across, he or she has to make a decision. That choice could be hard or easy, wrong or right, or for better or worse. In my case, many of the choices I've made turned out for the worse. I've been in and out of jail most of my life, so I could pretty much guarantee most of my decisions were not to my benefit.

So my story begins in a shopping mall. My ace, Spencer Thomas and I, were out shopping for a wedding band. I was finally heading to that alter. I never thought I'd see the day, but, suddenly, it was just three weeks away. God, I'd never been so excited. I was marrying this dame that I met on the internet. I met her on yahoo while I was doing a six month bid for violating my parole. We chatted on that computer for the entire time I was locked up. Man, she was interesting as hell, too. She liked to write, sing, and dance; you name it, she did it. I never met a woman so intelligent. And the icing on the cake was when we met face to face. Can you say knock out punch? Her complexion was tanned like caramel, with light brown eyes, sandy red hair, and nice plump lips with the hips to match. I knew when she picked me up from county, she was a keeper.

Now I don't want you to get the wrong idea. I wasn't whipped. But this girl, she was just too much to risk. I made a promise to her the first night we made love. I vowed to her that I'd never cheat or lie to her as long as I live. Now, considering all the women I had run through and how beautiful she was, I threw in my whole deck of cards and I closed shop. I submitted. In her case, she exhaled. That was three years ago, and I stayed true to my words to her. Now, I am a guy and my eyes do wander, but doesn't every guy's?

But just like I said, we were in the mall looking for a wedding band. I had a good job but it wasn't paying me exactly what I needed to get the kind of ring I wanted her to have. It was tough trying to find a descent job with the kind of record I had, but I had to make due with it.

"This is a nice one," said Spencer as he pointed at this platinum band.

"Man, do you see the price on that thing? Three thousand and... Wait, I'll stop there!" I shook my head.

"Make payments on it," he smiled.

It almost seemed like he was trying to be funny. "Whose gonna give me credit? Hello! I've been to prison a couple of times."

A salesman walked towards us. He was an arrogant dude; one of those types you could look at and tell has an attitude.

"Can I help you gentlemen?" he asked. He gave me a slight, 'nigga you can't be serious' smirk.

"Nah, we're just looking," I replied.

He looked down at the rings we were observing and smiled. "Ah, is someone getting married?"

Some pricks just don't catch on very quickly. "We'll call you when we need you."

Yep! I really pissed him off. His facial expression changed from the 'Hi, I'm fake smile' to the 'you have three seconds to get your black asses out of this store' frown.

"Well, if you gentlemen need some help, Lisa, at the register, will assist you." He walked away, staring out of the corner of his eyes.

"Spence, let's get out of here." We quickly headed towards the exit.

"So where to next?" asked Spencer.

"Let's get something to eat. All this shopping is making me hungry."

"But you didn't buy nothing yet."

"Like I said Spence, this shopping is making me hungry."

We walked down to the food court and jumped into the Burger Palace line. The line was long and my stomach was roaring like a lion. That's when Spencer's eyes picked up on something that I knew was trouble from the rip.

"Crap, Vic, check this out," said Spencer as he stared across the rows of tables.

I immediately turned around, "What?" That's when I saw it. Henry Hancock, father of my fiancé, snuggled tightly at a table beside a woman a third his age.

"Is she nibbling on his neck?" Spencer asked with his nose turned up.

"That's what it looks like." She was all over him in broad daylight. Her fingers danced up and down his shirt as he smiled, childishly fondling with the food on his tray. "Let's get out of here before he sees us."

"What?" replied Spencer. "Why?"

"Because I don't want him to see us."

Spencer giggled, "He can't do nothin' to you."

"Just come on," I said as I stepped towards the exit praying Mr. Hancock wouldn't spot me.

I drove swiftly down the street trying to grasp exactly what I had just seen. Spencer just stared at me, blushing. I tried valiantly not to look his way because I knew him well, and I knew he was thinking of an intricate scheme to make the incident a profitable one.

"So what are you going to do?"

"What do you mean, Spence?"

"Boy, you don't know you got a gold mine in front of you, do you?"

"Before you even suggest what it is you're thinking, no thank you!"

"What? You're not gonna tell nobody? Boy, black people just don't understand money." He shook his head. "You want a nice ring for the future wifey, don't you?"

I stared at him like he had lost all the seeds inside of that melon he called a head. "What do you want me to do, blackmail him or something? He's her father. I don't think so!"

"Well, you gotta do something!"

"Oh, I am. I'm going home and tell Brit. End of discussion!"

He yelled, "You're gonna do what?" He looked out of his window and grinned, "Lord, please tell me this nigga ain't say he gonna tell Britney?"

Maybe he was hard of hearing. "Yeah, I'm gonna tell her."

"Nigga, is you stupid?"

"No, I'm trying to do the right thing," I replied as I pulled into a parking space in front of his apartment.

"The right thang! Who the hell you wanna be, Spike Lee? The only thing doing the right thing is gonna do for you is leave your ass standing at the alter singing 'I wish I never met her at all', stupid!"

"Just shut up! Brit and I have trust. That's apart of our relationship."

"Boy, I tell you! You can't give an ex-con none and think he won't get whipped," he laughed. "She ain't gonna believe you over her father, fool! Nigga is you crazy? You know he's gonna lie and all she's gonna do is believe him. No matter what, he's the daddy and you're just some nigga she met on yahoo from the pen."

"Man, why you had to chop up our relationship like that?"

"'Cause it's the truth, Vic! You go to Brit and it's over-- end of discussion. But what you need to do is go to Mrs. Hancock, tell her what you know, and I promise you, no doubt guaranteed, you will be reimbursed!"

"But!"

"No buts! I have spoken." His eyes quickly jumped open. "I'll tell his old lady, her fine ass!"

"You're not telling her anything! Get out of my truck, too!"

He laughed, "Peace homey! Don't let that money truck pass you by, 'cause it did stop. Ya' better hop on nigga!" He jumped out of the car with that grin on his face. Damn that grin!

Out of all the shenanigans Spencer could come up with on the situation, he was right. If it were to come down between her father's word and mine, I would be the liar. And although I didn't want to keep anything from Brit because of my promise, this could somehow be beneficial for the both of us. Brit had only a little bit more cash than I had. She was one of those independent rich kids that didn't accept money from her folks when she got older. Mrs. Hancock was a respectful woman, and some sort of reimbursement from her would be inevitable. And I wouldn't even have to tell Britney. It would just come out in the open and Britney's mother could take it up with her father. We could just sit in the background unaffected. Instantly, my mind was made up. I was going to let the cat out of the bag and reep the benefits.

I smelled the sweet home cooking before I stepped foot into the house. Lord knows I could get use to that. My baby let herself in and was cutting a rug in the kitchen with Bob Marley pumping throughout the crib.

"Hey lady," I said as I did my little Rasta dance into the kitchen.

Her light brown eyes gleamed as a smiled erupted on her face, "Hey, baby, I didn't hear you come in." She sat her spoon on top of a pot and gave me a comforting hug.

Yes, I could get use to that fried chicken, black-eyed peas, collard greens and some of her for dessert every night. Just a few more reasons why my world revolved around her. I gave her a petite kiss on her cheeks. "You been here long?"

She quickly turned to her pot of greens and churned them. "Just for an hour. Mom and I were looking for another gown most of the day."

"What was wrong with the one you had made last month?"

"You know Mom; she wanted me in something a little trendier."

"Okay!" I scratched my head. "Who's getting married here?"

"Oh, Vic, don't be like that," she turned to me and wrapped her arms around my waist. "You know Mom never had a real wedding with Dad.

She's basically having hers through me."

I frowned, almost insulted by the whole ideal of what she said. "Yeah, but it's suppose to be about you!"

"Well, let's not forget, in the beginning it was about you."

I quickly pulled away from her and turned to the fridge. I opened it and grabbed a carton of orange juice. My throat was about to get dry because I knew exactly where this conversation was heading-- to my convictions. "Yeah, I should be happy your parents accept me now, even though I'm an ex-con."

"Vic...," she frowned. "Really, I wasn't going there."

"Well, I am," I firmly announced. "How can your mother be so concerned about the gown you're wearing for our wedding when she stopped talking to you for a whole eight months when you told her I was an ex-con? I don't buy it, Brit!"

"Now you know good and well that wasn't all Mom. Dad..."

"Yeah, I know," I sarcastically chuckled, "Your father was the real reason why she couldn't communicate. He gagged her in the basement of their big, pretty mansion."

"Geez, Vic, did you come home just to argue?"

Realizing I was beginning to make a spectacle of myself, I paused. By no means I wanted to argue with her. Besides that, once I told her mother about what I saw, Brit was going to be really hurt when she gets the news. "I'm sorry."

"Oh, Vic," she sadly shook her head, "She's talking now! She's even trying to get this wedding up and running and she's trying to be apart of our lives." She rubbed my chin. "Let's forget about what happened in the beginning and focus on the future. Now that my mother knows you, she knows that you'd never do anything to hurt me and that's all that matters to her."

I simmered down a little, but my pot of anger was still brewing in the back of my mind. "It's just kind of hard to forget what happened, that's all."

She smiled, "Well, we have to. It's the only way we can move on."

"How's your old man doing, anyway?" I quickly changed the subject to see if there were any signs of his descent going around.

"I haven't seen Dad." She added a little bit of salt to her collards. "Mom said he's been tied up at the office a lot lately."

He's been tied up, alright! "Your mom hasn't said anything about that?"

She grinned, "Of course not, Vic. She's been too tied up with the wedding. You make it sound as if he's cheating on her or something."

I quickly rebelled. "No, no, I was just concerned."

She turned the stove off.

"He's closing the deal on those grocery stores he just sold."

"Boy, your pops just keep making that money." I hope he has some left for alimony.

"I told you he offered you a job. He was talking about paying you a pretty penny, too."

Yeah, just another way he could tamper into our lives. "No thank you. I was flattered by the offer...."

"But you don't want to accept a job from my father." She rolled her eyes. "Vic, you've got to wake up. Everyone isn't getting those nice jobs the hard way. It's who you know, and my father is a very powerful man. Even if you don't want to work under him, I'm quite sure he could talk to one of his business pals and get you something you would enjoy."

"I'll be fine by myself." I grabbed her from behind and rested my chin on her shoulder. "I'll find something out there." I quickly dispelled Brit's idea of 'who you knew', and I became content with the ideal of 'what you knew'. And I knew something earth-shattering about Mr. Henry Hancock, and it was going to bring us a great deal of wealth.

The next morning I called in sick on my job. I made my way straight to the Hancock's estate. I knew Mr. Hancock carried those traditional business hours of nine to five, so I knew this morning would be my golden opportunity to make my move on Mrs. Hancock. It wasn't the fact that I didn't like the man. He was alright, although I could do without the arrogance his persona carried. He was just rich, and I needed just a little bit of what he had. I wanted to buy a ring for my baby.

I arrived on the front doorstep a little bit after ten. Mrs. Hancock's cherry red Jaguar was parked in their crowded circle of cars in the driveway. I knew she was home because the Jag was her favorite. It was her primary source of transportation, and it fitted her profile - high maintenance.

I rung the doorbell a couple of times so Mrs. Hancock would hear me. The cheap bastard didn't even have a butler. Ten bedrooms, two guestrooms, patio, game room, den, library, you name it, it was all jumbled into his mansion with no butler. If it were mine, I'd have a butler and two maids, all of 'em white. I'd legally changed their names and call on them for stupid stuff like turning up the television for me. I'd even...

"Vic?" uttered a voice.

It was Mrs. Hancock. Boy, it was Mrs. Hancock. She had her long, black hair down, wearing an oversized silky, black robe. Out of a scale from one to ten, she was a ninety-seven. Brit received all her looks from this lady.

"Can I help you, Vic?" she politely questioned.

"Oh, yes ma'am. Yes ma'am," I nervously looked around. "I just needed to talk with you privately for a moment. Are you alone?"

A petite smile appeared on her face, "Yes, I'm alone. I was just preparing to take a bath but I can make time for you. Come on in."

"Thank you, Mrs. Hancock," I replied.

"At," she raised her finger, "I told you about calling me Mrs. Hancock. I'm not an old woman, Vic. Call me Debra, please! Now come on in, it's a bit breezy out here."

I followed her inside of the classy crib. Jesus, if she wasn't Brit's mom...

"I hope you don't mind talking to me in the bathroom, but I need to start my water. I like my water to get settled before I jump in."

"No, not at all," I followed her through the trophy filled hallway. The walls were cluttered with medieval swords, shields, and paintings dating from the twelfth century on up. Her hubby loved to give ill-advised history lessons on the art he collected throughout the years. I know I've sat through about twenty lessons alone these past three years.

We entered their humongous bathroom. She started the water in the jacuzzi. It was blazing hot with the steam beginning to rise slowly towards the ceiling.

"So, Victor, what is it you wanted to talk to me about that is so private?" she said as she folded her arms and sat on the edge of the tub.

I was so nervous, I didn't know how to start. Her beauty was just so overwhelming and the thought of being alone with her with a jacuzzi accessible didn't help matters either. "Well Mrs.., I mean Debra, I ran up on some unsettling information."

"Unsettling?" she grew startled a bit. "Is Britney alright?"

"Yeah, yeah, this isn't about Brit," I quickly assured her. "Britney, she's fine, never been better."

"Okay?"

"Yeah, Britney, she's fine." Maybe I should've thought about how I was going to tell her. My heart began to thump, my palms were getting sweaty, and my throat began to dry.

"Victor?"

"Yes."

"What's the information?"

I decided to be a man about it and just go for it. "It's about your husband."

"Really." A stern look appeared on her face. "Did he try to offer you another job, because I told him about that?"

"No, not at all, Debra." Here goes nothing, I gulped. "I was out shopping for a ring for Brit yesterday." I sat on the toilet behind me. "He was cuddled with another woman."

"What?" She jumped up. "Are you sure, Victor?"

"She had her hand dancing up and down his chest as he just sat there and treasured her company. The chick had to be half his age, easy! She had nothing on you, though, really!" I tried to add a little comfort for her.

It wasn't like I was lying, though. Mrs. Hancock looked twenty times better than Henry's little side dish. It just made me wonder why us men do the stupid things we do.

Her eyes began to water as she stood before me with her head down. "Why would Henry do this to me?"

"I'm sorry Debra."

"All those late night meetings and weekend retreats were probably just a big front for his nasty, little escapades with his low class hoochies," she shook her head, "Certain times I've had feelings about him doing things he shouldn't, but my heart just wouldn't let me see it, Victor."

"I know. I know." I was lost for words.

"I mean, am I not attractive?"

"Yes. Yes, you are a fine woman, very fine." That was well understated.

"I work out everyday. I just got finished working on my abs. I keep myself up," she rambled as tears began to slowly race down her face. "Why would he do such a thing?"

"I'm sorry, Mrs. Hancock," I said as I gave her a soft hug. I never wanted to hurt anyone the way her husband did to her. But actions always spoke louder than words and I knew, in my past, I broke many hearts and told many tales. It's sad how easily us men break women hearts.

She laid her head on my chest and softly rambled explanations for her husband's infidelity. I simply looked up at the ceiling and asked myself why I had to be the bearer of such bad news. Was breaking a woman's heart worth a little bit of cash that I wasn't even promised? Was the money really worth being responsible for the breakage of a twenty-five year marriage? And as I continued to think I came up with my answer, yes! I needed what I needed and the opportunity presented itself. Henry Hancock was a stupid, rich bastard in my book and it was time for him to give up the kitty.

Suddenly, my feet began to feel damp. "What?" I quickly looked towards the floor. "The water!" Steam flooded the room as piping hot water overflowed the jacuzzi. I quickly let go of Debra and raced to the tub to stop the overflowing.

"Damn it!" I yelled as I drenched my shirt while I turned the knob to shut off the water.

"Vic," Debra softly called.

"Yeah," I answered. I turned around and my mouth dropped like the New Year's ball at Times Square. Mrs. Hancock stood before me with her robe completely off. Her caramel, plump breast and firmly, toned body revealed itself to me as if I was loose in the garden of Eden.

"Would you cheat on a person if you were coming home to this?" she asked with a confident smile on her face.

Hell no! "Uh, no, no ma'am," I stuttered.

"Then why do you think Henry does it?"

Stupid as hell, I guess. "I couldn't imagine why?" Spencer and his ideas. I was so nervous, I sat on the wet ledge of the jacuzzi. She began to walk towards me.

"Have you ever caught yourself looking at me Victor, almost forgetting that I would be your mother-in-law someday?"

"No ma'am." I was praying for lightning not to strike me down.

"Come on, Vic," she said as she stood in front of me and gently fondled with my ear. "It's just you and I talking. Now have you?"

"Well, Mrs..."

"Uh, uh," She placed her index finger on my lips. "It's Debra."

"Well, Debra, you know. My eyes... they've wandered occasionally."

She smiled, "I know they have." She placed my hand on her breast and slowly caressed herself with it.

What in the world was she doing, and why in the hell was I letting her do it?

"I've seen how you looked at me from time to time - your eyes following my breasts. Sometimes I've seen your eyes pop up after you glanced between my thighs."

"Debra, if you're trying to get back at Mr. Hancock..."

"Mr. Hancock is a dead issue. You've told me all I needed to know about my husband. And, no, I'm not trying to get back at him. I just want to get to know my future son-in-law a little better, that's all."

"Oh," I replied. What a way to get to know someone, I thought.

"Now, I need to know one more thing, Victor," she said.

"What's that, Mrs. Hancock?" I nervously cried.

"How good are you?" She shoved me into the tub, water splashing everywhere.

She jumped on top of me and planted me with a juicy kiss. At first I tried to rebel, but within seconds, I gave in. She ripped my clothes off and I accepted my unexpected reimbursement.

I woke up to the eerie echo of the jacuzzi's dripping faucet. I jumped out of the tub, grabbed a towel and dried myself off. I looked around for my clothes and Debra; neither were in sight. I wrapped the towel around my waist and proceeded to the exit. Suddenly, I heard the television blasting down the hall near the den. That room quickly became my destination point.

My mind rapidly flooded itself with thoughts of losing Britney as I walked down the hall. I couldn't help but wonder what would possess a mother to have sex with her daughter's man. My excuse was simple; I was a man and I was sorry like that. But sleeping with my fiancé's mother, I didn't know if the dirtiest of dogs would do that.

I approached the den. Immediately, I saw Debra sitting on the couch watching Oprah. She still had her robe on, hair up, curled up on the sofa, chewing on celery sticks. My clothes were neatly folded beside her on the arm of the sofa.

She blushed as I entered the room. "I dried your clothes for you," she smiled. "They were drenched quite badly."

I stared at her, trying to understand how her mind was working. She was acting like we didn't do anything wrong. "How long was I asleep?"

"About an hour and a half. I didn't want to wake you. You were sleeping so peacefully."

"Debra, about what we did…"

"Between you and I, forever."

"But why did it happen?"

"I have my reasons, Victor. Don't think I'm not apologetic pertaining to the circumstances because I am. I would never do anything intentionally to hurt my daughter. So you shouldn't try to suddenly become the heroic hero-man with all the morals and think that telling her about what we did would be the right thing," she smiled. "I know my Britney. We'll both lose. You more than I, my dear boy."

"But…"

"My husband will be home within the next hour. I think you need to start getting ready."

"So that's it?"

"What more can there be, Victor?" She jumped off of the sofa and approached me. "I thank you so much for the information you've given me. But when it comes down to you and I sleeping together, no one pulled your arm, and no one pulled mine. We mutually committed to doing it, leaving us both at fault. No one must find out, or the world as we know it will come tumbling down."

I simply stared at her, knowing she was right on point. If anyone found out about what happened, everything would be ruined. How could I be so dumb? There was surely no extra money coming into my pockets. I didn't know what possessed me into thinking that in the first place. The circumstances led me to a huge disappointment in myself. Every time I went to jail, it was because I followed behind someone else's advice or business. With this situation, I was gullible to even consider anything coming out of Spencer's mouth. I grabbed my clothes, got dressed and left. She didn't even see me out.

Frightened as hell to go home because I knew Brit would be there, I ended up at Spencer's place. He had no full-time job, so I knew he'd be there.

"What is it?" he swung his front door open, rubbing the wake-up out of his eyes.

"It's me, ass!" I replied.

He still had his pajamas on while it was pushing close to six in the evening. The wonderful benefits of putting your grandfather's inheritance into a mutual fund.

"What you want?" He asked as he stepped aside and let me in. "I was sleeping good as hell!"

"Wake up, I need to talk to you."

He shut the door behind me. "What? You got that reimbursement for snitching on Mr. Hancock?

I rolled my eyes. "Something like that."

"Really? How much she gave you?"

"Some legs and thighs."

"Man, she gave you chicken?"

"No ass! She gave me sex!"

"Whoa!" His eyes quickly widened. His perverted grin sprang on his face. "You banged Mrs. Hancock!"

"Don't be so loud!" I said not wanting the whole world to know.

"You hit that? Got-dog!" he laughed, "Was it good?"

"I don't know!" I turned away from him while frantically shaking my head. "What does it matter if it was good or not? I slept with my fiancé's mother for goodness-sake!"

"Dag, that is messed up!"

I turned and frowned at him. "Is that all you can say? This was your bright idea."

"Well..."

"If it weren't for you, I wouldn't even be in this mess. You have to see everything in the mall, don't you?"

"Wait a minute, slappy! I didn't make you sleep with Brit's mom, although I would've strongly suggested it, if I knew it was gonna be possible," he laughed.

"You see! You're just not on my level, are you?" I couldn't believe I actually sought refuge in Spencer.

"Well, dag, man, I don't know what you want me to say." He looked to the floor and shook his head, clearly thinking. "You better not let Brit find out."

"How can I not? I never kept anything from her, Spence."

"Well you better start now, nigga! She finds out about this and you'll be solo like O.J., and nobody wants to be in that nigga shoes. How did you pull off knocking off Mrs. Hancock anyway?"

"I didn't try anything!"

"What? She just gave you the nappy?"

"Well, I just turned around for a second and she was naked."

"What?" He burst out in a pathetic laughter, "I knew she was a nympho!"

"Can we please change the direction of this conversation?" I said as I became intensely frustrated by his sex-crazed comments, "I mean, I need some help here. What am I going to tell Britney?"

"Nothing, you jackass!"

"But I can't lie to her."

He smiled and took a deep breath. "You love her?"

"Yes!"

"You want to marry her?"

"Yes!"

"Will she leave you if she knew you got your freak on with her mother?"

"Hell yeah!"

"Well take it from a man who has had many years of experience with lying to women - don't tell her! Also, don't look in her eyes while talking to her for a good three weeks."

"What?"

"Don't look in her eyes when you're talking to her! Women are like special agent cops or something. They can tell if something wrong just by looking in your eyes. So don't risk it. Talk to her with your head turned," he laughed, "Women got this sixth sense thing where they can make a nigga tell the truth just by looking in his eyes. You'll say something stupid, telling on yourself."

I looked at him puzzled by his information. "Spence, how do you know so much about women without being in a relationship with one?"

"Exactly! I know so much about 'em that I don't need to be in a relationship with 'em."

Thanks to Spencer, I was determined not to look in Brit's eyes when I got home. "Thanks, Spence!" I reached for the doorknob to leave his apartment.

"Hey!" he yelled.

"What?"

"Between you and me... never mind!"

"What is it, Spencer?"

He giggled, "Okay.... Was it good, man?"

"Uhhhh!" I screamed as I stormed out of the house and ran to my car. Good ole' Spencer, couldn't keep his mind out of the gutter for a good three seconds.

The ride home took forever. Maybe it was just the fact that I couldn't drive no more than twenty miles per hour. As I sat and feared the confrontation ahead of me, I came to a startling revelation - I was whipped! That explained why I feared talking to Brit. Long ago, I could lie to a woman with the straightest face, but not with Britney. It was so important to me how I was perceived in her eyes. Since she came into my life I stopped cursing, drinking, and lying. And, suddenly, I found myself back to my old tricks but this time, in the presence of a woman I so dearly loved.

I walked into the house and saw her sitting on the couch reading some Terry McMillan. She loved her some Terry.

"Hey baby!" I walked into the den.

She quickly looked up and blushed. You could see the excitement take over her whole body with her smile, "Hey boo!"

All it took was a split second for me to turn away from her. My God, what have I done, I thought. I knew I was going to end up breaking down in front of her.

"How was work?" She sat her book aside and walked to me. She hugged me and gave me a small peck on my lips.

I couldn't even kiss her the same. "Fine. Just fine," I said as I pulled away from her.

She looked puzzled, "Vic, are you alright?"

"Yeah, yeah," I replied, denying my discomfort. "Why'd you ask that?"

"I don't know, you seem a little tense."

"Really? I'm alright. I'm cool."

"Would you like for me to give you a massage?" She put her arms around my neck and stared at me. I quickly looked away, trying to avoid any eye contact.

"No, not right now. I actually need to use the bathroom," I pulled her arms from around my neck and quickly charged into the bathroom.

I didn't have to use it, I just had to get away from her. I sat on the toilet and stared at the ceiling. "What the hell did I do?" I questioned myself.

"Boo, I made some broccoli casserole. It's on the stove," she said from the other side of the door.

"Thanks, babe, I'll get some when I'm out of here."

"Okay, I'm gonna stay over here tonight. I'm too tired to drive," she said.

"That's cool, baby. I'll see you in the morning." I tried to sound normal. "I just have a little upset stomach that I have to take care of right now."

"Goodnight, boo!"

"Goodnight, babe. I love you," I replied.

"Love you, too."

Nervous as hell, I knew I couldn't stay in the bathroom for three weeks, or whenever Spencer said the lie-face wore off. But I understood what was at stake, so I knew longer work hours would have to be key. My conscience was shot, and I had to find a way to ease it. At least on my job I could forget about the Hancock's and the lie I was keeping from Britney. It was just me and my urinals.

"Hey, Vic, telephone!" screamed my boss as he wobbled his fat, midget-self into the bathroom.

I was on my knees trying to tighten the bolts on the bottom of a toilet. I never understood what business guys ate for lunch but it sure paid off for hours. "For me?" I replied, a little shocked to get a call at work.

"Here," he handed me his cell phone. "Whoever it is called you directly on my line. Don't be giving out my number, no more! I handle's my business on that there line!"

"I di...," I stopped myself realizing I didn't even know his cell number in the first place. I just grabbed the phone. "Hello?"

"Victor?" said the voice.

It was Henry Hancock on the other end. My heart raced as terrifying thoughts fluttered through my mind. Did he know?

"Mr. Hancock," my voice cracked.

My boss, knowing very well who Henry Hancock was, walked a little closer to me so he could ease-drop.

"Yes, Victor, I was wondering if you could stop by and see me after you got off from work?"

"Ah, I don't know what time I'm getting off today, Mr. Hancock. I have an awful lot of jobs to do today."

"Well it doesn't matter what time you get here. I just need to speak with you briefly, dear boy."

I was greatly intrigued. "It can't be handled over the phone?"

"Now, Victor, you know I'm a businessman. I feel that business should never be handled over the phone."

I smiled, "Uh, so this is business? What kind of business are we talking about here?"

"Be here at six sharp, dear boy. You'll find out everything then."

"But..." Before I even got the rest of my sentence out, he had already hung up his phone. The nerve of that guy, telling me where I needed to be, and when I needed to be there. Oh well, I needed to find out what kind of game he was playing and what was this meeting all about. Lord knows, rich people are crazy.

I returned the phone to my boss.

"Oh, you finished already?" he asked acting as if he wasn't being nosey.

"Yeah, I'm finished."

"Well, hey, tell Mr. Hancock that Lou asked about him when you see him at six."

"Will do, Lou. Will do!" Poor people were just as crazy, though.

I arrived at the Hancock's estate around seven o'clock. I knew Henry didn't like me, so there was no need for me to impress him by being courteous and on time. Debra's car wasn't parked in the lot, so I knew it was just me and Henry.

I rang the doorbell and it was almost like he was impatiently waiting for me to ring on the other end. He opened the door immediately.

"Ah, Victor," he grinned. He was wearing his usual, custom made, three-piece suit, with his hair slicked back as if he were a white man trying skillfully to hide the baldness at the center of his head.

"Mr. Hancock," I said as I shook his hand.

"Do come in."

It always surprised me how some black folk could come out of the deepest ghetto and when they get a little bit of money, everything changes about them, from the way they walk to the way they speak. Mr. Hancock was no exception. He was the whitest black man I knew.

"Thanks, Mr. Hancock." I walked in as he closed the door behind me.

"Follow me, please." He led the way down his huge hallway. "You have to excuse all the dust on my toys, I haven't had a chance to do any dusting lately."

"It's cool. You ought to see my car," I said just throwing something out there.

He gave me a 'where does that fit in' glance. "Ah, the car. Yes, indeed."

We walked into his office.

"Have a seat," he directed me to the chair in front of his desk. He sat behind the desk.

The office was huge and cluttered with a lot of old books. On one wall, he had three medieval swords displayed. He once told me the swords were actually used in a few Roman battles. Like I really cared.

"So, Henry, what's the deal?" I said arrogantly. I figured if he knew, there was no need to prolong the agony.

"What's the deal. Your generation kills me with that kind of lingo," he grinned. "Actually, there's no deal, Victor. I just wanted to share a moment with my soon to be son-in-law."

"So that's all you want? No more job offers, no nothing. You just wanted to chat?"

"Well... yes." He stood up. "I realized what my wife and I did to you and Britney in the beginning of your relationship was unfair and I just wanted a chance to patch things up."

"Really, Mr. Hancock, there's no hard feelings. Forgive and forget, that's what the Bible says."

"Yeah, the Bible," he grinned as he looked towards his prestigious swords. "You read the Bible a lot, Victor?"

"Well, I turned to it every time my cases went to court. I read it a little while I was locked up."

"Some interesting things in it, don't you think?"

"Of course." I began to wonder where the conversation was heading. Hopefully it was just leading to another one of his rambling sessions. I could deal with it as long as he knew nothing about me and his wife.

"I was always fond of the ten commandments. My favorite one is the one that tells folks they shouldn't steal."

"Really?"

"Yes, really, Victor," he smiled, almost in a trance with his swords. "You know, Victor, when you're a rich man a lot of folks think you steal from others to get what you have. They think rich men are bad somehow. Do you agree with that means of thinking?"

"No, not all. Being rich shouldn't determine if you're a good or bad person. It should be determined on your actions, not your wealth."

"Exactly Victor!" he shouted as he looked at me and smiled. "It should have nothing to do with it!" He bowed his head. "You know, Victor, my claim to fame was through being a bad person. Before I owned all my companies and real estate, I sold life insurance."

"Really?" Yeah, he was going on to ramble for a little while, which meant I was in the clear. I decided to sit back and happily be his little earpiece for a while.

"Now don't get me wrong, not all insurance salesmen are bad. Most of them are good human beings. It's just the information you gather from being in the business. You see, Victor, there's two type of life insurance; term and cash value. Term is good and cash value is bad; not a lot of people know that. Now for a long time, black people, say you and I, could not purchase term insurance. It was illegal for a salesman to even offer it to us. They sold us cash value policies, most not being worth anything when our folks passed and didn't do much financially for the next generations. It basically didn't do anything for our community. It simply benefited the salesman by giving him or her a higher commission."

My butt began to quickly get numb from the chair. I was hoping his speech would end soon.

"So when I got my start in selling insurance it was legal to sell both policies to black folks. And black folks were my biggest customers, and guess which policy I sold to them?"

"Ah, term," I answered.

"No. I sold them cash value policies."

"Really!" I always knew he was a crook.

"Yeah, the commissions were much, much higher. I made a killing!"

"I bet you did." I prayed to God he would shut up and let me leave.

"Do you think that made me a bad man, Victor?"

"Well, it's hard to say. You had to feed your family, right? But it's not good that you had that type of information and you didn't help the community with it."

"Information!" he snapped. "By God, Victor, you're a genius. Information is the most powerful tool in the world. But see I didn't use that information properly. I used it to benefit myself and not for the higher good. Why, I could have gotten our people policies that would enable them to stop working when a loved one died, but I didn't. I just did what benefited me!"

"Exactly!" My eyebrow raised a little because it seemed that his conversation was about to take a deadly turn for my worse.

"Now let's get back to the part of the Bible that discusses stealing. Now it states that, 'Thou shalt not steal'. Technically, I've stolen before, me simply not offering a better policy to my own people. Why, that's stolen opportunities. Are you following me Victor?"

"Yeah, sure."

He looked me straight into my eyes. "I bet you didn't know that some historians speculate that Augustus Caesar knew he was going to get sabotaged by Brutus?"

"Ah, no, Mr. Hancock, I never heard about that." History buff, not I.

"Indeed! Some folks suggest he knew about the plans for his demise. But I know different. I know for a fact that he didn't know anything simply because it's in a man's nature to take precautions when troubles are abound."

Just a little bit longer, I suspected.

"Victor, you ever wonder why I don't have any butlers or maids in such a big house?"

I smiled.

"You're blushing. What is it?" he asked.

"Well, Mr. Hancock, no disrespect, but I always thought you were just being cheap," I laughed.

He laughed along with me. "That's cute, Victor. It does save money, though, believe me. But there's another reason, old boy." He once again turned to his swords and rubbed the blade of the middle one. "You see, Victor, I had a friend once."

Wow, he had a friend. Couldn't have been one of the corpses he sold life insurance to.

"He was my best friend in the world, old Walter Wilber. But something was going on. He'd stay for weekends and suddenly things would disappear. First, just some china, then some silver, then valuable paintings. Frankly, I was getting ripped off quite badly."

"Wow," I replied.

"Debra and I, we hired new butlers, new maids, but our things continued to turn up missing. So that's when I drew the line. I decided to do something Debra didn't even know about."

"What did you do?"

He smiled at me and faced his swords.

"I got sneaky." He took the middle sword off of the wall and stepped back. Suddenly, the wall revolved from inside-out, into a group of television monitors. "I had cameras installed in every single room, every little place I could cram one in.

Oh my God, I thought. I couldn't move. I just froze.

"The next weekend he stayed with us, I had the evidence and information to prove that good old Walter Wilber was the one ripping me off. I made sure he paid the price, too. After that, I got rid of the butler and all of the maids. I didn't trust anyone," he smiled. "Now, do you see how powerful information is when you use it correctly?"

"Yeah, of course," I mumbled.

He walked to his desk and sat down. His eyes didn't leave me. "It seems you had a little bit of information that you didn't seem to use correctly."

He pulled out a remote from under his desk. He turned on all of the monitors. All of them showing me walking down the hall with Mrs. Hancock.

"Middle-aged men go through this thing they call mid-life crisis."

My eyes stayed glued on the monitors, as I was too scared to even twiddle my fingers.

"We have to do certain things to keep us from thinking about getting old. We have to find ways to lie to ourselves. My way, same as a lot of others, is to find a chick half my age, easy. Didn't you say that?"

I was angered as I continued to view the tape. I made love to his wife and he knew it.

He shut off the monitors, "No need to see the rest. We both know what happened."

"What do you want me to do?"

"Calm down, Victor. There's no need to get so tense. Like I said on the phone, this is business."

I looked at him, puzzled. "What?"

He stood up, "That's right, dear boy. This is certified business!"

I sat back in my chair, completely baffled.

"You see, Victor, I like you. You take risks. Why, you can't be rich if you don't take risks," he grinned, "Now I guarantee you, you thought Debra was going to give you some kind of payment for the information you gave her. Am I right?"

"Yeah?" I hopelessly nodded my head.

"She paid you alright, just not what you intended. Correct?"

"Yeah."

"But little did you know, if you needed some money, all you had to do was come to me. You see, Victor, the world summed up in a nutshell goes like this - you either do or you don't. You do use the information you have correctly or you don't. And if you mess it up, you may get another chance to do it right."

I simply waited for the part of the speech to come where he demanded me to get out of town. I would most definitely be doing that.

"Now what I will do, Victor, is give you another chance."

"Now why would you do that? I slept with your wife and cheated on your daughter."

He shook his head, agreeing with me, and returned to his chair. He placed both his elbows on his desk and grinned, "That's true, but I'm going to let you do something to redeem yourself to me. Simply because, Victor, when I found out that Walter Wilber was the crook stealing my goods, I also found out he was sleeping with my wife. Her stock value was down long before you even came into the picture."

"Really?"

"So, do you really love my daughter, Victor?"

"Yes. I love her more than anything in the world."

He smiled. "Well, I guess murdering her mother wouldn't be too much to ask of you, will it?"

"What?"

"That's right, dear boy. I want you to kill the deceitful bitch!"

"Are you serious? I can't kill your wife!"

"Oh yes you can. I even got it planned all out for you."

I jumped up and backed away from his desk. "Hancock, I'm not a murderer. I know you know about my record, but that's a whole different ball park. I won't even consider doing something like that."

"Oh yes you will, Victor. If you want to marry my precious little daughter, you most certainly will. I've even decided to throw in three million dollars for you."

Suddenly, the whole tone of the environment changed. "Three million dollars!" My God, was he insane? I slowly returned to my chair.

"Think about it, Vic, three million dollars, the girl of your dreams, and no bitching mother-in-law," he said. "All you have to do is show up here tomorrow night for a little nookie and strangle the broad."

At first, I didn't believe my ears, but suddenly I couldn't believe I was considering doing it. I just sat there with the idea of being rich beyond my wildest dreams and sharing my wealth with the woman I loved.

"So are you game, son?"

I looked him in his eyes, still in my little trance, and I nodded my head. "Yes, I'll do it."

He chuckled, "Great! I knew you would do the right thing, Victor."

My stomach churned as I became instantly disgusted with myself. Out of all the crimes I committed, none of them were violent offenses. Now it had come to this, seconds away from being in a plot to commit first-degree murder.

"I want you to do it tomorrow night. Debra will be here all alone. She thinks I'm going out of town in the morning on a business trip for two days. Quite naturally, with the information you gave her the other day, she'll think I'm on a rendezvous with my little companion on the side. And that's where you'll come in, dear boy!"

"How?" I listened eagerly while I doubted my own sanity.

"You will come over, around nine. She'll be eager for any form of company. And you, you'll basically do what you did the last time, just be here, and she'll eventually come on to you. Now, I don't care how you do it, but the first opportunity you get, I want you to put her to rest."

I looked at him like he was out of his mind. "That's your plan? You don't have a certain way you want me to kill her? Just do it?"

"It doesn't matter how you do it, Victor. As long as it's done," he smiled. "The next morning, I'll come home early, discover her lifeless body somewhere in this house and call the police."

"What about my prints and stuff like that? There will be an investigation. That's just too risky."

"If you want to wear gloves, fine. I have this town's police department in my back pocket. I'll simply tell them certain things were missing and it'll be classified as a robbery that went terribly wrong. I won't pressure a full investigation, and that'll be the end of it."

I suddenly became highly objective against the whole idea. "So you think you have it like that with the police department?"

"Victor, I am this town's police department."

I scratched my head as his words danced around in my brain. I knew he was a pretty powerful man, but did he really have that much pull? Even though it would be a high profile case, he would be my buffer. Why me anticipating marrying into the family, there would be no way I would even be implicated for the crime. If they would look at anyone, they'd look at him. And with the results of so many sketchy, high profile cases in the past, it's evident that rich men easily buy there way out of trouble.

"One question, Mr. Hancock?"

"What is it?"

"Where will you be while I'm over here murdering your wife?"

"I'll be at the Holiday Inn with our alibi."

"Our alibi?"

"Yes, dear boy. We'll both need one of those. See, my chick on the side, as you so eloquently defined her. If and when the question of our whereabouts come up, it will be discovered that we were in a casual meeting discussing your new position as a business manager for one of my apartment complexes. We were discussing your role and salary requirements over some drinks. All questions will be taken care of."

Suddenly, his sketchy plan looked quite appealing. "It sounds good but the money, how will I explain that to Britney? You know she doesn't like cash handouts from you."

"Yes, my daughter always wanted to prove to me she could make her money on her own. I have this friend that does these sweepstakes. I'll make arrangements with him to make it look as if you won the money through a phony contest," he grinned. "Nothing's impossible when you have money, dear boy."

He was so right. God, I never disliked anyone as much as him, but he was giving me a golden opportunity to get what I needed to live the lavish lifestyle I always dreamed of.

He extended his hand. "So is it a deal?"

"Yeah, it's a deal." I shook his hand.

Fearing reneging on the plan Hancock and I designed, that night I called home and told Brit I had some late assignments to finish at my job. I told her not to wait up for me. Not wanting to be around anyone, I simply drove around the city most of the night. When I did come home, Brit was knocked out. The next morning I felt her gentle kiss on the side of my face before she went off to work. I pretended to be asleep, knowing I hadn't slept one wink the entire night. I didn't even show up for work that day. Hancock and I figured it would work for my story if I didn't show up on my job that day, just to make it seem like I quit. I just laid in my bed, sadly contemplating what would be the easiest way to murder Mrs. Hancock - strangling her or just a plain ole' whap upside her head.

Around eight, I arrived at the Hancock's estate. It was nice and dark out so I knew no one would see my car. It didn't matter much because the mansion was a good three or four miles away from anyone else's home. As I spotted her cherry red Jaguar, I knew it would be just me and Debra, just like Hancock stated. I sat behind my wheel, took a deep breath and gathered all my thoughts. I had to compose myself and stay calm. I exited my car and headed for the house. I decided to come in strong, so I firmly knocked on the door. A few seconds and suddenly the door swung open.

"Victor," Debra answered, surprised. She was equipped with a bottle of wine, wearing slacks and a blouse that was opened midway, revealing a little cleavage.

"Hi, Debra. How are you?" I replied, trying to act normal.

She smirked, "I didn't expect you to come by today."

From the smell of things, she had been drinking for a little while. Her breath reeked! "Well, I just dropped by to talk for a little bit. Can I come in?"

"Sure." She stepped aside as I entered the house.

As I walked in, I glanced at every wall in the room, contemplating the number of cameras recording my every move.

"How's Britney?" she asked.

"She's fine."

"Come along, I'm upstairs in the game room." She made her way upstairs, I followed closely behind. "I haven't called her in a few days, you know? I don't know how I should talk to her," she sighed.

"I know exactly what you mean," I replied.

She stopped walking halfway up the stairs and slightly turned to me, "Do you?" She shook her head and continued to the top.

Her stare stunned me for a moment as I continued to follow her. We entered their leisure room. The room was exquisitely furnished with a marble pool table, big screen, digital television, a fancy sixties jukebox and Italian leather sofas. She walked to the window and stared out of it as I palmed a pool ball and juggled it with one hand.

"I know what you thought when I opened the door with this bottle of wine in my hand. The broad finally lost it, right? Her guilt has taken her over the edge, right?"

I placed the ball on the table, "No."

She turned around grinning, "Victor, I slept with my daughter's future husband, of course you thought I was feeling guilty. But needless to say, I wasn't. I felt good about what we did. Lord forbid if Britney should ever find out, but it really felt good."

I didn't know if I should've felt flattered or put her out of her misery right then and there. There was no way in hell I was going to feel good about what we did. Especially after doing what I had to do to her, "About what we did..."

"Henry's on a business trip for the next two days. I know he's probably somewhere shacked up with his little fling-thing, though." She took a big gulp from the bottle, "I hope he's enjoying himself."

"So he left you all alone?"

"Yes, he did," she approached me, "If he only knew about the hours of steamy sex you and I had in his luscious jacuzzi."

"Hopefully, he'll never find out!" I dug into my pocket and felt around for the shoe string I brought along with me. I wanted to get the job done fast and simple. As much as I enjoyed having sex with her, I didn't want to do it again.

"Oh, he's too stupid to suspect anything. He thinks my world revolves around him." She took another gulp from the half-empty bottle. "He wouldn't know if I was sleeping around, if I was having sex with someone right next to him in the same bed! And you know, I needed some good sex for a change, because with him, it's just ten minutes and lights out. I really don't know what that little tramp sees in him besides his money."

Was she really that dumb? Only if she knew the secrets that laid in the house she slept in.

"He's a pathetic moron!" she laughed as she took another swig from the bottle.

I pulled the string out of my pocket and palmed it.

"But you," she placed her hand on my cheek, "You're so different. I figured that the only reason you have the background you had was because of the wrong choices you've made. If you only thought about the things you done before you done them."

Suddenly, I froze. I looked into her eyes and I saw Britney. It was like the love of my life was speaking through her. My God, what was I doing? She pulled her hand away from my face and suddenly she burst into tears.

"Debra?" I said. "What's wrong?"

"I'm a bad woman!" she cried. "I slept with my daughter's fiancé!"

"Ohhhh," Rapidly, chill bumps ran through my entire body as I grabbed her and hugged her tightly. "No, no, no, don't cry. Look, we're in this together."

Suddenly, I dropped the shoe string on the floor, not caring about where it landed. I contemplated murdering another human being, something I never thought I was capable of doing. Tears slid down my face as I became ashamed of the man I had suddenly become over the course of the past few days. I knew then, that the wedding Britney and I had so eagerly planned for, would never take place. I most certainly had to reveal the truth to my love as soon as possible. I had been such a fool. Henry Hancock could keep his money because I was no murderer!

Unexpectedly, I heard the faint sound of a car door slamming. "What the…"

I released Debra and slowly walked towards the window. Several police cars were down below, with their lights flashing. The officers quickly exited their cars and ran towards the house. Mr. Hancock's blue Suburban pulled into the driveway also. What the hell was going on, I thought. He wasn't suppose to come back until tomorrow.

"Oh Victor!" yelled Debra. I quickly turned around.

She smiled and violently smashed herself over her head with the wine bottle.

"Hey!" I screamed as I ran towards her falling body. "What the hell is wrong with you!" I caught her before she fell. I gently laid her onto the floor. Her head began to bleed profusely as I held her in my arms.

"Don't move!" yelled a black officer, bursting through the door with his gun pointed at me.

"Whoa, whoa, wait! Get that gun out of my face," I yelled.

"Get away from the body, asshole!" yelled a white officer that came from behind the black cop.

"Hey, man, you guys need to chill out for a moment," I yelled as I gently laid Debra's unconscious body on the floor. I raised my hand and slowly backed away from her.

"Up against the wall!" the white cop yelled.

I simply followed directions and turned to the wall with my hands up. The white cop immediately grappled me in cuffs. Obviously, there was some sort of misunderstanding. "I don't know what's going on, but you guys are making a big mistake. I didn't do anything to her."

The cop turned me around as the other cop quickly jumped to Debra's aid.

"She knocked herself over the head with a wine bottle," I stated.

"Yeah right, jerk!" said the cop as he tightly grasped my elbow.

Oh my God, they thought I attacked her. "Whoa, I didn't do anything to her."

Suddenly, Mr. Hancock burst through the door with the paramedics behind him. He quickly looked towards his wife's body on the floor. "My God!" he yelled, almost in tears.

"Henry, man, what's going on?" I yelled frantically trying to understand the situation.

He quickly looked at me with his eyeballs bulging out of his skull, "You animal!"

"What the hell! Man, what's wrong with you? Why are acting like you didn't set this up!"

"I knew you couldn't be trusted."

"What?" I screamed. This fool was going nuts.

"I don't know what my Britney saw in you, but now she's going to see the truth," he yelled pointing his finger in my face. "You're going away for a very long time, mister!"

"That's for damn sure," yelled the cop as he pulled me through the exit with him.

"My darling!" Henry cried as he tried to jump over the paramedics to get to his wife.

"Henry, what are you doing?" I hopelessly screamed.

The officer escorted me down the stairs and out to a police car.

I sat in the car for a good forty-five minutes. The ambulance quickly rushed Debra to the hospital twenty minutes earlier. The Hancock's yard was swarming with cops and news cameras everywhere. There was even a helicopter that shinned it's bright spotlight on the car I was in the entire time.

It all too clearly became evident that the Hancock's set me up for some reason, and I somehow figured it was Britney-related. With such a brilliant scheme, they must've been planning it for months.

Henry stood in the middle of a gang of officers a few feet from the car I was sitting in. He whispered something in one of the officer's ear, and, suddenly, he walked to the car they were holding me in. The officer opened the front door and Henry jumped in. It was just him, I, and the gate that separated us.

He looked down and smiled to himself. "You didn't see it coming, did you, dear boy?"

Mad as hell, I just stared at him.

"Did you really think I was going to let you marry my Britney, inherit my fortune and have jail bait, bastard children with my daughter? Did you really think I was going to let that happen? No, dear boy, I don't think so. I knew it wasn't going to work the minute Britney brought you home to us."

"So you really didn't want me to marry her? This is what all this is about, me and Britney? You and your wife..."

"Will do anything to get what we want, dear boy!" He turned and smiled at me. "You see, I didn't lie to you about the philosophy of what makes up this world. You simply misunderstood."

"When I get out..."

"Oh, you will never get out!" he smiled. "You will rot in prison."

"I'll tell them everything."

"You don't have a pot to piss in! Catch all the sights your eyes can gather because this is all the outside you will ever see for the rest of your useless life!" He opened the car door. "Good-bye, Victor."

He exited the car and returned to the huddle of police officers. Out of the corner of my eye, I saw Britney run pass my car. She quickly ran to her father and embraced him tightly. She let go and turned around, looking straight at me. I could see in her face that she was mad as hell. Tears slid down her face as she slowly pulled her engagement ring off her finger and dropped it on the ground. Her father placed his arm around her waist and they walked to his truck.

I knew then that Henry and Debra Hancock had won. They managed to take the only thing away from me that ever mattered - my Britney. Oh, how quickly I realized that some things are meant to be told and some are meant to be kept secret. And when I think about it, rich people are crazy. But so are poor folks like me!

The End

Ghetto Eyes

Ever since his first time on the court, he was called the man.
When it came down to the wire, it was up to him to make his game expand.
Killer cross-over with a nasty jump-shot;
No one else dared get the rock when Jo Jo was hot!
But after the arena lights went dim,
Something very sad happened to him.
No longer was he handling that orange rock with those black stripes.
He had enough of playing games once he started tooting on that pipe.
But everyday in the hood, this is getting to be no surprise;
Just a little glimpse of this world through my ghetto eyes.

She was nice and thick, the baddest of any red bone ever seen.
Oh how Levi's complimented her when she wore those skin-tight jeans.
But in eighth-grade she had no intentions on learning from any books,
Just lying on her back, low-riding with all them older crooks.
By the tenth, she was pregnant with her second baby.
Her mother raised her and her kids, the whole neighborhood called her crazy.
And as time progressed, she discovered she had full blown AIDS,
And all that trickin' she did ran constantly through her mind during her final days.
But everyday in the hood, this is getting to be no surprise,
Just a little glimpse of this world through my ghetto eyes.

Ricky graduated valedictorian, the highest spot in high school.
While everyone was out partying, Ricky's home studying, he wasn't no fool.
He studied and studied, got himself a full scholarship,
Went to college, continued to do well, even got involved in a relationship.
The love of his life, taught him all about love, and brought sex to his doorstep.
In his bed, on campus, is where they had relations and where they both slept.
But one night, around three, standing over his bed was this cat named Jerry.
He blew both their brains out; poor Ricky didn't know she was married.
But everyday in the hood, this is getting to be no surprise;
Just a little glimpse of this world through my ghetto eyes.

Why am I here?

Why am I here, trying to make a dollar out of fifteen cents?
Could've stayed in bed, sleeping at my own expense.
Ain't no bills in my dreams,
Just an ass of money and high self esteem.
Pardon my French, but everybody curse.
Talking crap or eating it, you choose which is worse.
But that's beside the point,
Let me clock out and we'll both roll a joint.
Come back to the this mutha' high as hell the next day,
Get high together, to hell with minimum wage pay.
And when the smoke of the bud turns clear,
We'll both be asking, why in the hell are we here?

The Pimp, The Ho, The Consumer

The pimp, the ho, the consumer.
She better have my money, and it best be tonight.
She come here with another excuse, I'm just not gonna do right.
Gave her so many chances, put her at the top of my squad.
But she couldn't even go through her first job, like that was so hard.
Why my mother was a ho, and all her sisters led the way,
So she better bring me my money, and she best bring it today!
--The Pimp

The pimp, the ho, the consumer.
I don't know how I ended up in this world that's so crazy.
First it was just dancing, now it's this, just to feed my baby.
But at least I'm getting paid; most girls give it up and later on get played.
And I used protection every time, so I know I don't have AIDS.
But sometimes, when they're on top of me, and I'm fading everything out,
I think about my past, the mistakes I've made, knowing I should try another route.
And some nights, I don't feel much like living,
Like there's another part of me dying from this thing that I'm giving.
--The Ho

The pimp, the ho, the consumer.
I'll teach her, acting all stingy with the nappy.
Sometimes I think she had that kid just to trap me.

Well, I guess I have nobody to blame but me.
But she don't have to give it up, I'll find someone else to satisfy me.
And to hell with it, if I should catch some kind of disease.
You win some, you lose some; I'm just out to be pleased.
--The Consumer

One day

One day I'll wake up, won't have to hear shots bangin'.
On the neighborhood block, there won't be no drug slangin'.
I won't have to be scared to get pulled over by a cop,
And that white lady won't be watching me so closely when I shop.

One day I'll wake up, my generation, not worrying about the threat of AIDS.
I could get a job, not have to worry about minimum wage pay,
And that darn flag in front of that dome would no longer be an issue,
And every state will give Dr. King his well deserved tribute.

One day I'll wake up, my brothers won't be pulling me down like we're a bunch of crabs,
And my brothers upstate could finally catch a cab,
And one day all this could happen, never again would my bliss hopelessly fall,
Or will this just be the one day that I don't wake up at all?

Evolution

Alright now, boy, I want you to pick all that cotton.
After that, fetch them pears off the ground; you keep the ones that's rotten.
And don't get lazy, Ron's watching your every step.
But you a good boy, won't run away like those that did last night as I slept.
And you will be rewarded, my hardest working boy yet!
Now gone do what I told you, and don't you forget.
Yes 'sa, yes 'sa boss.

Boy, I want you to shine these here shoes, shine 'em nice and bright.
I wanna see 'em sparkle from the reflection of a candle light.
Do as I say, and you'll get this nice, hefty quarter.
And I apologize about last night, I didn't know she was your daughter.
Why she looked at me, came on to me, knew very well what she was getting into,
And I'd never rape one of your people, that's something my race would never do.
But get on and shine, boy, I got places to go, like the store.
Once again, I'm sorry you ended up raising a little, black whore.
Yes 'sa, yeah...

Boy, that was a close one, I thought we were almost done.
It's okay you came in at three, even though I scheduled you at one.
But just try to be on time a little more 'cause I got big plans for you;
And keep your eyes on everybody, let me know what these folks are up to.

My boss says he wants you to follow the flow, and do a little for him;
Your promotion will be inevitable, and your raise far from slim.
So do what you gotta do, and we'll show you all the ropes,
And there won't be anymore projects for you and no more selling dope.
Yeah, man, whatever!

For Sale

We can sit a night and talk about the wrongs and rights of the community,
Argue and complain about everything we think the white man's doing unjustly,
Even parade and march, screaming out unity.
But does it really matter if we go out to eat and look down at those folks serving us,
Ignore the issues of fellow workers because our noses are so far up the boss's butt,
See those same workers get discriminated against, but pretend the references weren't to us,
Get a little bit of cash and all the sudden there's no need to make a fuss.
It would be nice if our issues weren't for sale,
If everybody could get raises and the boss-man could still go to hell,
If everyone could tip in, when another brother fails,
And everyone could say in unity, "No, this race ain't for sale!"

Lil' Miss Shady

Gone, girl, with your bad self!

Saw me enter the room and you straight up left.

I know he's your man, but I ain't gon' say nothin'!

You think I was gon' tell him you offered me some of that stuffin'?

No, girl, I wouldn't cramp your style.

But you could've said something to a brotha', maybe crack a smile.

But you didn't, just blessed me with the cold shoulder--

Knew you would act different 'round your man, see I told ya'!

Talking 'bout how you wanted to break the bones out of my back.

But, Lil' Miss Shady, you think I want some of that after seeing how you act?

You liable to get a nigga in some big-time trouble.

And you ain't all that, hate to bust your bubble.

So gone on, walk off with your jive-time man,

'Cause if I could get it that easy, then I guess anyone can!

Banking on it

I walked in, thirteen cents and a check in my hand.

One-fifty, for all that work, they trying to drag this man.

Light bill due, rent and the cable,

They don't even have a pen at this table.

"Excuse me, do you have a pen I can borrow?"

"Thank you!" Damn, I need to come in early tomorrow.

Baby-momma gonna be buggin' me 'bout some cheddar.

I owe Doris some loot, too, but I ain't gonna sweat her.

Good, I'm next in line.

For that child support, I'm gonna need a little more time.

Boy, I wish I had enough dough for them shoes in the mall.

But with all these bills, this lousy check couldn't cover it all.

"Can I help you sir? You're next."

I guess those will have to wait 'til my next check.

"Yeah, can you cash this?"

And I owe Trey, but that nigga's a wuss.

"Okay, I need two forms of I.D."

That nigga better not come to my house sweatin' me!

Damn, I need to ask to work some more days.

They straight up acting like they can't give me another raise.

All that work I do, I bust my butt in that joint!

But with all these bills, and this small check, what's the freakin' point?

"One hundred and fifty dollars, will that be all for you today?"

Huh, what the hell did that broad say?

"Excuse me, what did you say?"

"I asked, would that be all for you today?"

"Uh no, actually I need something else from you."

"Well, what is it that I can do?"

I always thought about doing it, so it's gonna feel funny...

Ah, here's my pistol, "Trick, give me all your money!"

It was you…

Daddy, it was you that told me wrong from right.
Told me that whatever I wanted, for it, prepare to fight.
Stick my chest out, never turn my back on a foe.
If someone set up a blockade, then I gotta knock down the door.

Daddy, it was you that taught me how to treat a lady.
Don't hurt 'em, just love 'em, no matter if they acting crazy.
Love just one, put her on the pedestal and let her know it.
And times may get rough, but that comes with the package.
And don't listen to negative friends; how far did they get with that racket?

Daddy, it was you who showed me what being a man is all about.
If things ain't going the right way, you told me to try another route.
And not too many of my friends had someone like you on their side,
So when I say I love my daddy, I say those words with pride.

Indifferences

Well get mad!
You're the one that's been had.
Talking all that mess, trying to act ill.
Have we forgot just who pays the bills?
Okay, okay, I didn't mean to shout.
Baby, please don't make me sleep on that couch!

Sweet ole' Carolina

What could be finer?

First to stand up and secede from the Union,

Last to find out sins can't be paid off through communion.

The land where yesterday and tomorrow looks about the same;

A place where whole-hearty Americans find considerations somewhat hard to obtain.

What could be finer?

Where else could you go today and see a symbol that represents hate,

And go back about a hundred years prior and see that same symbol of hate;

Buy barbecue from a white supremacist as he dictates the art of slavery,

And display his banner of hate and be glamorized for his chivalry?

What could be finer?

Why nothing could be finer than sweet ole' Carolina.

And those who complain about it are just a bunch of whiners.

We were the first to secede and we never came back,

And you still don't amount to the capacity of one white man if your color is black.

Ms. Mystery Woman

Ms. Mystery Woman,
The one that walked into the club last night,
The lady that was wearing that outfit that was so damn tight,
The dame that made them two brothers at the bar, straight knuckle up and fight.
Yeah, blackberry pie with them slanted eyes,
I was that brick-hard brother that you just couldn't pass by.
Made you stop, stare and ask yourself why?
Why can't a pass this Negro by?

Ms. Mystery Woman,
It was I, who took you on that dance floor and made you flow to the beat,
It was I, who made your eyes stay glued and fixed it where you forgot how to speak.
Yes me, sexual chocolate from my head down to my feet.
If you had a man, you forgot him, because you were straight up ready to cheat.

Mr. Mystery Woman,
You entered my house like you were the world's gift since your birth,
But it was I and my flyness that brought your fine ass back down to earth.
My image plays back and forth, up and down, in your pretty little mind,
A brotha' with an ego as large as yours and your luscious behind.

Ms. Mystery Woman,
Next time you come to my palace, you better beware,
Come with something a little bit tighter, and, this time, wear some underwear.
Then get on your knees, and say a little prayer that I won't be there,
Best regards, from that nigga that broke you down, Mr. Mystery Player.

Is You?

Is you the dude I grew up with?

Is you serious about curling your hair with that kit?

Is you trying to walk like you have no arch in your back?

Is you trying to say most people in the ghetto smoke or deal crack?

Is you trying to talk in that high-pitched tone?

Is you trying to say you don't wanna talk when you don't answer your phone?

Is you saying me and you can't be friends no more?

Is you trying to say for your tastes, I'm too poor?

Is you forgetting where you came from?

Is you dating that chick 'cause she white, even though I heard her say you was dumb?

Is you understanding my ghetto monotone?

Are you trying to tell me to leave your wannabe as---pirations alone?

Hated On

My Brother,

Big, black brother,

Brother, brother, brother,

Why'd you step on my shoes?

Why'd your lip drop when you heard my good news?

I thought we were down like four flat tires,

That your heart was with me, no matter what transpired.

That, about you, is what I most admired.

But I was hated on!

Often contemplated on.

Almost regulated on.

Like Augustus, your knife almost severed my back.

Like Jesus, I knew somewhere there was a rat.

You hatin' on me, I just couldn't picture that.

But it was true, you were shady like a pine tree.

You were out for self, never mind me.

Can't believe I had someone like you beside me.

Anticipating my demise,

Lust and hatred all in your eyes.

All on the cost of my surprise.

You were my brother,

Big, black brother,

Brother, brother, brother.

When It Comes Around

She lie in bed, in a trance, with the beaming red, digital clock. She awakened so many times before the alarm went off. Waking up fifteen minutes early this morning was nothing unusual. It just ticked her off a little. She simply stayed put and enjoyed the morning silence.

Suddenly, her husband, Clyde, rolled over and faced her. While observing his nappy beard, she smiled. His eyes cracked slightly open. Awakened, he batted his eyes, surprised that his wife was staring at him.

"Damn, you look rough in the morning!" he uttered as he quickly turned opposite of her.

She frowned, her feelings obviously hurt.

"Fix me and the boys some pancakes, too. I feel like some pancakes and eggs this morning," he said as he squirmed on his pillow to get comfortable.

She stared at the clock with her mouth wide open, "I gotta be at work in an hour!" Brenda announced.

"Well, you best go on and get started," he griped, "I ain't going no where hungry! Go on and wake them boys up, too. Get 'em dressed so I can take 'em over to Momma's house."

She pouted and grabbed her robe beside the bed. She quickly slung it on her firmly built physique and stomped into the bathroom.

"His lazy, no-good ass!" she said as she grabbed her toothbrush. She applied some toothpaste on it and began to violently brush her teeth.

The alarm from the bedroom scattered it's annoying siren throughout the apartment.

"Why in the hell didn't you cut this goddamn thing off?" screamed Clyde from the bedroom.

She spit out her toothpaste, smirked, and slammed the door shut. A loud crack could be heard from Clyde throwing the alarm against the wall--his morning ritual. She wiped her mouth and observed her teeth. Staring at her own flawless, caramel-tanned face, she suddenly paused.

What did I get myself into, she thought. It became her daily routine to ask herself this question in the morning for the past seven years. She looked down at her belly and gently rubbed it. She sadly shook her head as she reminisced about her reason for being in her current situation.

She had gotten pregnant at the tender age of seventeen. While in high school, she was hot in her pants and regular, high school boys were just too immature for her taste. She had her sights on being with older men. They had more to offer and could get into places young boys couldn't. She met Clyde, and he was mature and had a lot going for him at the time. He was a well-known mechanic with his own shop.

Their relationship was in trouble from the very beginning, with Clyde being twenty-eight, but she didn't care. She had to have him because he was a man, a real grown man. Of course, things soured when she discovered that she was pregnant and on top of that, Clyde was a "real" married man with two kids. Things worsened when Clyde's wife, Sharon, found out about the affair and tried to run her over one day while she was walking from school. Sharon missed her by inches and collided into a tree, killing her instantly.

How easily your mistakes could flash before you every single day, she thought as she rubbed her belly. She married Clyde a month after his wife's accident and lost her baby six months after that. She was going to name the girl Mary, just like the mother she had never met.

"Open that door, I gotta piss!" yelled Clyde as he violently beat on the door.

She quickly opened the door as he rushed right by her and pulled his drawers down, releasing his juices into the toilet. She just stared at him.

"You started breakfast yet?" he turned to her while urinating.

"I'm about to fix it now," she replied.

She exited the bathroom and entered the bedroom. She grabbed her work clothes out of the closet along with the ironing board. She turned on the television with the remote as she plugged the iron into the wall. She flicked the channels trying to find the right one. She stopped at the morning news.

"Three more robberies occurred last night on the south side," said the news anchor. "Police believe that not only were the three connected with each other last night, but they are all in conjunction with a string of seventeen robberies this month. Descriptions of the suspect are sketchy, but he is believed to be a black male, approximately six feet tall with brown eyes. Although there haven't been any violence during these robberies, police believe the suspect is armed and dangerous..."

"Sounds like my type," smiled Brenda as she ironed her shirt.

"You ain't fixed them pancakes yet?" asked Clyde as he stood in the doorway with his hands on his waist.

She slammed the iron down. "I'll fix 'em right now!" she said as she rolled her eyes and walked out of the bedroom.

"Alright!" Clyde yelled. "Don't be rolling your damn eyes at me. I'll knock 'em out!"

She entered the kitchen and quickly cut on the stove. She opened up a cabinet under the sink as roaches scattered everywhere. "Damn it!" she yelled as she backed away. "Nasty roaches!"

She grabbed a frying pan and dumped it into the sink. She poured a half bottle of detergent in the pan and scrubbed it clean with scolding hot water. Roach infestation was never her steelo because her grandparents didn't play that.

Twenty minutes later, the food was ready. The boys Deshawn and Travon, both sat with their heads on the table. Brenda simply sat their plates above their heads, not wanting to wake them, knowing how disrespectful they were to her in the morning.

Clyde walked into the kitchen, buttoning up his shirt. "Alright, y'all, wake your little asses up at that table!" he yelled.

The children's head quickly rose.

"Hey, daddy!" said Deshawn, the youngest of the two.

"What's up, little man?" smiled Clyde as he took his seat at the head of the table. "Travon, boy, what's wrong, cat got your tongue?"

The ten year old frowned, "Brenda won't fix me no grits!"

Clyde yelled, "Boy, what I told you about that? You don't call her Brenda. You call her momma!"

Travon sadly bowed his head, "Yes sir."

Brenda stared at Travon, pleased that Clyde had finally stood up for her.

Clyde quickly turned to Brenda, "Fix the boy some grits."

She frowned. "Grits! That's gonna take fifteen more minutes!"

Deshawn and Travon giggled.

"Woman, I don't wanna hear no lip out of you today! Fix my boy some grits!"

She sighed and opened the cabinet, reaching for the container of grits.

Clyde looked around his plate, "Where the syrup at? Give me some syrup, too, Brenda," he said as he buttered his pancakes.

She tucked her shirt down her pants in front of the mirror. She was already twenty minutes late, but no one at her job ever expected her there on time knowing about the situation she was in.

The phone rang. She looked towards the phone. It rang again as she charged to it and picked it up.

"Hello?" she answered.

The person on the other end was there, they just weren't saying anything. She heard their breathing loud and clearly.

"Hello?" she answered again, "Who is this?"

The caller hung up. Brenda shook her head and slammed down the phone. The phone suddenly ran again. She just stared at it.

"I got it!" yelled Clyde from the kitchen.

Brenda sighed and sat on the bed. She knew it was a female. She remembered back when she first met Clyde and how she used to not say anything on the phone when Sharon answered. Often times, she would call Sharon a bitch before hanging up, thinking she was doing something big. How wrong she was.

"If you ready to go to work, you better come on!" yelled Clyde from the kitchen.

She quickly jumped up, "I'm ready!" She ran out of the room, into the kitchen.

The boys were putting on their coats as Clyde stared at her, disgusted by the sight of her. "I ain't never seen nobody that happy to go to work."

"Can we go, please? I'm already late." She walked towards the door.

"You bet not be cutting out on me with none of them young children at your job! 'Cause if I find out something, it ain't gonna be nice."

The boys smiled.

"Can we go, please!" she said as she walked out of the house.

The boys and Clyde followed her out. The boys and Brenda jumped into the beat up station wagon.

"Hey!" screamed a voice.

Clyde looked over to the apartments next to his. It was Slim.

"Nigga, what you want?"

He had no shirt on, showing his lanky chest, while standing beside his broken-down, '84 Chevy Cavalier. "Man, when you gonna fix this car for me? I can't fix this damn thing! Jay says the timing belt needs changing, but I done fiddled with that thang and fiddled with it."

"Well, I'll probably leave the shop early today. Boss man been cutting back on hours. I'll come check it out today. Don't mess it up no more. I ain't gonna be fucking with that piece of junk all night."

"Alright, Clyde," he smiled. "I appreciate that!"

"Later," said Clyde as he jumped into the car. He started the car and drove off.

They pulled into the Chicken Coop's parking lot. Brenda quickly gathered her things and opened the door.

"Damn, you ain't gonna give a nigga a kiss before you rush out of here?"

She sighed, leaned over and gave him a quick kiss. He smiled.

"Boys, tell your mother, goodbye."

"Bye," the boys sluggishly replied.

She didn't reply as she jumped out of the car.

"Hey," yelled Clyde.

"Yeah," she said as she slammed the door and bent down.

"I love you," he smiled.

She frowned, "Love you, too."

She backed away as he drove the wagon out of the parking lot and down the street.

She entered the restaurant. The place was packed with folks scrambling to get breakfast. She immediately noticed Lonnie working the front register struggling to keep up with the orders. He was the manager. She hated working with him because not a moment went by when they worked together that he wasn't suggesting getting into her panties. He was black as coal, nappy head, with his belly abundantly sagging over his belt. In the employee meetings, when he didn't say anything, his breathing resembled a motorcycle streaking down the highway a few miles away. She often wondered, who would lie down with him, willingly? She certainly wouldn't.

She rushed through the kitchen door and stood behind him. "Clock me in," she said as she shoved him out of the way.

"Oh, now you come in. Thirty minutes late," he said, "You must be take me for a freaking joke or something."

"Shut up and clock me in," she replied as she smiled at the next customer in line. "Welcome to the Chicken Coop, may I take your order?"

"Hey, Brenda, how are you doing this morning?" replied the customer. "I'm not done with you yet! We'll talk later on." Lonnie angrily stomped to the back of the restaurant.

She smiled, "Will you be having your usual, Frank?"

"Yeah, let me get that, will ya?"

Brenda and Anita stood in the window at the drive-thru. Finally there were no customers around. They both knew it was just the calm before the storm. At noon, it was a whole different ball game-- lunch.

"Girl, let me tell you what this nigga called himself doing last night," said Anita as she leaned on the register.

"What he do?" asked Brenda as she rinsed out a coffee pot in the sink.

"This nigga call himself coming home at three in the morning. Talking about he got off work late."

"Don't he work for UPS?"

"Yeah, first shift, too! You know what, girl, I didn't even get mad, since he is taking care of Larry's baby. He just don't know it's Larry's yet.

But still, ain't nobody gonna try to clown me in my house, you know I mean girl?"

"Yeah, I know."

"I just want the nigga for his money. UPS do pay good, too. His little trick on the side can have 'em, 'cause I know where his check is going-- right home to mamma, girl!" she chuckled, "Shoot, I got my own on the backburner, anyway."

Brenda filled the coffee pot with water, "What's going on with you and Ricky, anyway?"

"Oh, he tired too!" she smirked. "Do you know I ain't even gave this nigga none yet, and he already talkin' 'bout marriage? How played can you get?"

Brenda nodded with a puzzled look. The things Anita complained about, she envied. How she wished she could find a man that wanted a real commitment, without sex being the most important thing in the relationship. The idea of being with a man that was also a friend was her only true dream.

"Brenda, you got a customer," said Anita as she strained to look over the counter. She smiled, "It's your man, Miguel, too!"

"Really?" she replied, startled.

Anita laughed, "You better take that man's order before I go over there."

Brenda quickly made her way to the front register.

"Offer him a side of nookie, too," Anita whispered.

Brenda gave her a dirty look as she stood behind the register.

"Hi, Miguel," Brenda said nervously.

Anita watched, sipping through a straw with her jumbo-sized diet drink.

"Hey, Brenda, how are you today?" asked Miguel. He was tall, light-skinned, with a goat-tee.

"I'm fine, just fine. Will this be for here?" she nervously asked as she grabbed a tray.

"Yes, Brenda," he smiled, "That's a question you shouldn't have to ask. I enjoy staring at you from afar while eating my lunch."

Brenda blushed, "What can I get for you?"

"A one-way trip to the Virgin Islands, accompanied with you!"

She laughed, "Yeah, right! You're so sweet, Miguel."

Anita rolled her eyes and began taking an order at the drive-thru.

"I wish I could go away on an island," said Brenda.

"Why can't you?"

"What? I don't have any money, Miguel," she laughed, "So what will you be having today?"

"Give me that chicken-shack snack you guys offer."

"What kind of drink?"

"Fruit punch," he answered, "You know, money is only an object. It should never be something that holds someone back from doing what they truly desire. There are other means of achieving your dreams."

She smirked, "There's not many without the need of money. Besides, I don't even dream anymore, Miguel," she stated as she fixed his order, "I damn near don't have any money at all, and my marriage is all but perfect. So what is there to really dream about?"

"Your honesty is the essence of your beautiful personality," he said.

She smiled as she fixed his drink. "Here you go, Miguel." She handed him his tray.

Lonnie walked onto the front line and observed the two.

"Thank you, Brenda," he smiled as he walked away with his tray. "Talk to you later."

Lonnie quickly took post directly behind her. "Any man that smiles all the time is a liar," he whispered in her ear, "There's something Mr. Miguel is hiding, know what I mean?"

"Why don't you try and hide that big gut you got rubbing against my back?" She backed away from him, "And don't be walking up on me like that! What's wrong with you?"

"Why you always gotta front when it comes to us?"

"Lonnie, there is no us!" she argued. "How would you like it if Clyde came up here and put his foot up your behind?"

"Clyde, that punk! I use to terrify that clown when we were in grade school. Well, when that nigga came to school. Besides, that bum don't give a rat's ass about you no ways. Remember Candy that use to run drive-thru?"

"Yeah."

"Well he's poking that! That's why she quit. She didn't want no drama from you."

"What," she frowned, "How do you know?"

"Hell, your man ain't keeping no secrets," he grinned, "What makes you think he changed since he got with you, anyway?"

She was clearly upset, "I'm going on break!" She grabbed a sandwich from under the sandwich station and placed it on a tray.

"You can't go on break right now. It's almost lunch time!"

She fixed herself a drink at the fountain dispenser. "Watch me!" She walked off of the front line and entered the dining room.

He looked towards Anita who was giggling. "You don't have nothing better to do but stand there?"

She frowned, "Oh shut up!" She grabbed an ice bucket and strolled to the back of the kitchen.

Lonnie faced the dining room and stared at Brenda as she took a seat by the window. "I'll get ya' sooner or later." He walked to the back and entered his office, slamming the door.

Brenda sat in front of the window, staring at the cars rapidly passing by. She drifted into thought, thinking about the proposed trip to the Virgin Islands Miguel had jokingly offered her. The thought of being away from Clyde would be a dream come true. She vibrantly remembered the one time she did muster enough gut to walk away from her dreaded marriage to Clyde. It was that night she came home from work and found a used condom beside the toilet. Obviously, he thought he disposed of it after he had a sexual encounter with some hoochie, but he had somehow managed to miss the toilet, leaving it lying on the floor for her eyes to discover.

They argued for hours. Clyde proclaimed he had left his brother and his girlfriend at the house while he was out looking for another job. But it only turned out to be a lie because his brother was in jail that day and had been for about three weeks prior. No, she caught him red-handed and she knew all her grief was finally over. She was leaving him.

She stormed out of the house and headed for the car. That's when Clyde did something she had only heard rumors of him doing in his previous marriage. He grabbed her by the back of her hair, forcing her off her feet and dragged her into the house. He slammed the door shut and pounded on her face. Knowing that outside, folks saw him dragging her into the house, she screamed for help but ironically no one came to her rescue. Clyde had quite a reputation for being a notorious thug, and no one dared come between him and any dispute. No one even bothered to called the cops. He beat her bloody for about fifteen minutes. Her nose was broken, her lips swollen, and she sustained four broken ribs. He took her to the hospital afterwards and told the doctor she had fallen down the stairs at his mother's house. She agreed, conscious of the fact that if she didn't go along with the story, only more violence awaited her when they returned home. She thought only one thing was more upsetting than getting beat by her husband; it was the fact that his two boys witnessed it all.

She sat in front of the window with a tear sliding down her face, just about squeezing the meat out of the bun of her sandwich. She was a nomad in sadness.

"You alright?" asked a voice.

"Huh," she uttered as she abruptly parted from her thoughts. It was Miguel.

"Brenda, are you okay?" he asked as he stood before her with his tray in his hands.

She quickly put on a fake smile, "Yeah, sure, I'm okay." She wiped her eyes.

"Well, can I eat my lunch with you?"

"Ah," she looked around, instantly thinking about her warning from Clyde that morning about her interactions with other men, "I don't…"

"Thank you," he said as he took the chair beside her. "I've been waiting so long for you to come out and sit with me."

She blushed, "Well, you've only been coming here for a few weeks, Miguel."

"Four weeks," He took a sip of his drink. "It's been the longest four weeks of my life, waiting for your company out here."

She smiled, "You're such a dream, Miguel."

"No," he pointed at her, "You said you didn't dream anymore. Make up your mind now."

"I said, I didn't dream anymore, and that you were a dream! That's two different things."

He nodded his head. "Okay, I'll let you slide this time," he smiled. "So what's to matter. I couldn't help but notice your demeanor a few seconds ago."

"Oh nothing," she grinned, "Just thinking about some mistakes I've made."

He chomped on his chicken leg. "The only way you can truly learn anything about life is by making mistakes, Brenda."

"So have you made any mistakes, Mr. Perfect?"

"Oh yeah," he laughed, "I make about a hundred of them a day. But I learn from each one. Why, if I could roll back the hands of time, I would've fled my apartment in Los Angeles and came out here and swept you away a long time ago."

She blushed, "You're such a smooth talker. So, really, are you from L.A.?"

"Well, I lived there for about five years. I'm originally from Seattle. I moved down to California right after college, thinking that I was going to find me a job through that infamous American dream! How wrong was I."

"What did you major in?"

"Film."

"Really?"

"Yeah, I was going to be the next Spike Lee!"

"Wow!" She took a sip from her cup. "Why did you stop pursuing that dream?"

"Well, I wanted to bring realistic images of blacks to the screen, but the Hollywood execs just weren't having it. They weren't interested in putting real or different images of our culture on the big screen They just wanted those darn black gangster flicks. And there's so much competition out there that's trying to give it to them."

"Well, you shouldn't let that turn you away from your dreams."

"Oh I didn't," he smiled, "Instead of creating a movie in Hollywood, I turned my life into one big movie. This is the part where I meet the girl."

"You're so funny! Really, what do you do now?"

"I live this movie I call my life, Brenda. I just travel from town to town and gather all my experiences and collect them on my notepad. Once I've experienced enough things, I think I'll give Hollywood another try. With the story I'm writing now, I know they won't turn me down."

"Well that's pretty amazing Miguel. I wish you the best."

"What about you, Brenda? What do you want out of your movie?"

"My life ain't even a movie. And if it was, it'll be a horror," she paused and thought for a moment. "All I want is happiness Miguel. It's been alluding me for so long that I don't know where to search anymore. Somehow, I confused it with coming here everyday, but I truly dread this place. I can't stand being around food, I despise my manager, and I hate waiting on people. Yet, I keep coming back. I hate my marriage, but I keep coming back. I..."

"You need to take control of your destiny." He gently placed his hand on top of hers. "All you have to do is stand up and shout at it. Tell it to come here, and let's ride the hell out! Don't let anyone or anything stop you from riding out with your destiny, Brenda."

A tear slid down her face, "How do I find destiny, Miguel?"

"Sometimes it finds you, beauty," he smiled, "Sometimes it finds you." He wiped his hand on a napkin and dried her eye.

"Look at me, getting all emotional." She looked towards the door where a crowd of people were heading inside the restaurant. "Lunch is about to kick off, and I'm out here crying. That slob back there is liable to come out here any minute and bless me out. I better get back to work."

"Yeah, you don't want any trouble out of him."

She stacked all her trash on her tray and jumped out of her chair. He quickly grabbed her hand.

"Hey, don't be afraid of anything. Find that destiny you're searching for and scream at it!"

She blushed, "I'll do something. Bye, Miguel." She dumped her items into the trash container and entered the kitchen.

She stood her post behind the front register, staring at Miguel from behind. Lonnie quickly stomped onto the front line.

"Son of a bitch!" screamed Lonnie.

"Why are you cursing up here? Customers are out there!" She quickly faced him.

"That bastard robbed three banks this morning!"

"Who?"

"That damn guy that's been robbing everywhere! His ass robbed three banks around this block in a twenty minute time span and got away this morning. Now, everybody on night shift is calling in!"

"What?" she replied.

"I ain't staying late," yelled Anita in the middle of taking an order at the drive-thru. "So don't even ask!"

"And Bill called in, too," he shook his head. "Now I gotta run a double by my damn self! Why, I wish that jackass would try to rob me tonight! I got something in the back of that safe that will light his ass up! I've been waiting on something like this."

She sighed, "Look, Lonnie, I'll stay with you tonight, but you have to keep your hands and your disgusting comments to yourself."

"Really? You'll stay?"

"Did you hear what I just said?" She gave him a stern look. "The second you try and get fresh with me, I'm leaving!"

"Alright, alright! It's a deal."

"Now, can you please stay up here and help us pack these orders that are about to come?"

"Yeah, sure," he said as he grabbed a pair of tongs and prepared to take orders.

Anita sat down at the table grappling a cigarette out the side of her mouth as Brenda wiped tables. "Girl, you know you crazy for staying up here by yourself with Lonnie. Then we got that robber going around here holding up every place he sees."

"That robber ain't even thinking about the Chicken Coop. We don't make enough money at night."

"That's why you need to go on home. 'Cause you know Lonnie's gonna try something on you."

"He better not! Child, I'll knee him so hard in his nuts..."

"What nuts? That fool probably ain't seen his equipment since he been crawling on all fours, his fat ass!" Anita laughed, "I know you don't like going home, but don't stay here with him, girl. Not tonight, it's too dangerous!"

"It can't be no more dangerous than staying home with Clyde, him and his up and down attitude."

"Girl, why you put up with it? Just leave that nigga. Or kill him!"

Brenda laughed, "You know you're crazy, don't you?"

"I ain't playing. Kill that nigga!" She took a hit from her cigarette, "Girl, I be begging for a nigga to hit on me, just one time, any nigga. I'll beat that man so bad, he'll never hit again! You see, you gotta let a nigga know. Ain't no man gonna hit you if you set him straight."

"He doesn't hit me often, Anita."

She put out her cigarette as she noticed her ride pulling into the parking lot outside. "Once is enough. I'll beat his ass. You want me to beat his ass, girl?"

"No! Girl, go 'head home before Trent leaves you. I just saw him pull in out there."

"Ah, that nigga ain't going nowhere! He better not leave me if he want some of this tonight." She pointed down at her crouch as she stared through the window. "But let me get out of here before the bank closes. He's gonna give me some dollars today, talking about being out all night. I'll fix his ass! Bye Brenda!" She rushed to the exit.

"See ya, girl!" she replied.

Brenda wiped her last table, stared at all of them, and rested her fists on her waist as if she conquered a tremendous feat. Lonnie approached her from behind and placed his hand on the small of her back.

"I see you finished the dining area," he said.

She immediately jumped away from him, "I told you not to walk up on me like that, didn't I?"

Lonnie sighed, "Oh, go ahead. I wasn't trying to do nothing. I was just checking up on you. I called my regional director and he gave me the green-light to lock the dinning room two hours before closing. I didn't want any of them suits to creep up here tonight and wonder why the doors are locked 'cause they are getting locked early tonight."

Not really moved by his comments, she rolled her eyes, "Well, the sooner we have them locked, the quicker we can close this store."

"Right! Well, I'm gonna be in my office. Holler if you need anything. We'll probably be dead until around seven anyway, so that'll give us a three hour break."

"Alright," replied Brenda as she grabbed a seat at one of the tables.

"Cool," said Lonnie as he walked away and entered the kitchen.

"See ya, Brenda," said Sammie, the chicken fryer, as he stood by the exit.

"Oh, see you later, Sammie," replied Brenda.

"Hey, I told Lonnie, that last batch of chicken I dropped should last y'all a while. It ain't that busy up in here at night."

"Okay, Sammie. Thanks," said Brenda as she gazed out of the window.

"Bye," Sammie exited the restaurant.

Suddenly, Clyde pulled into the parking lot. Travon jumped out of the car and ran into the building. He looked around for a moment.

"I'm over here, Travon," she raised her hand.

He walked halfway to her, "Daddy said come on!"

"Tell your father that I'm working a double today, and I'll need him to pick me up at ten instead of now."

Travon sucked his teeth as he walked towards the exit, "Alright," He swiftly marched out of the restaurant and returned to the car.

She stared out of the window, anticipating a reaction from Clyde. Immediately, his door swung open and he jumped out of the car with the other boy. They all headed into the building.

"Oh Lord," she sighed.

Clyde stormed into the building, looking mad as hell. "What you mean you need me to pick you up at ten? Why you ain't call me to let me know this? You got me out here wasting my gas," he argued as he trampled to her table.

"Clyde, no one's coming in tonight, so I told Lonnie I'd work a double with him."

"What the hell that got to do with me?" Clyde turned his attention to the kitchen area. "That fat ass need to do some work for a change, anyway! And why the hell you ain't call me to let me know all this?"

"Because I just found out!"

"What?"

"I just found out, Clyde," she rephrased her answer a little nicer.

Clyde frowned, "Well, the boys staying here with you."

"What?" Brenda and the boys replied simultaneously.

"That's right, they're staying here with you!"

"Man!" mumbled Travon.

"Boy, what?" Clyde looked down at him.

"I ain't say nothing," Travon quickly reneged.

"That's what I thought you said!" Clyde faced Brenda, "After I get finished working on Slim's car, me and the fellas are going out and getting a few drinks. If I ain't here by ten, here go some money for a cab." He threw a ten dollar bill on the table before her.

She shook her head, "You're not even planning on picking me up, are you?"

He squinted his eyes and grinded his teeth, "Take the damn money before you be walking. I don't want my boys walking nowhere."

She leaned back in her chair and laughed, "I was so gullible to think things were going to be any different for me."

He bowed his head, "Boys, y'all don't act like no fools in this here place tonight. If you do, you know what y'all can expect."

"Yes sir," the boys replied simultaneously.

Clyde gave his wife one last stare as she turned her head. He stomped out of the restaurant.

Brenda turned her attention to the boys. "I want you guys to sit over there in the corner." She pointed to the far corner, away from the entrance. "Let me know if you two get hungry." She stood up.

"Don't tell us what to do," said Travon as he sat at the table.

She gazed at him with a smile, "You know, Travon, I'm not even going to waste my time with your little attitude. Do whatever you wanna do." She walked to the door.

"I'm gonna tell daddy you was mean to us," he cried.

She ignored his comments and entered the kitchen area. She grabbed a towel off of the counter and began wiping down the shelves. "Lord help me. It's going to be a long night." She stopped wiping the shelves for a moment and stared at the boys walking around the dining room, knocking over every chair they came across. She sighed and shook her head.

The seven o'clock rush had come and gone. The boys sat in the dining room munching on some chicken strips. Lonnie was leaning over the front counter thumbing though a magazine. Brenda sat on a crate at the drive-thru scrubbing the walls. It was a long, boring night.

Brenda threw her towel down and wiped the sweat off of her forehead. She turned around and stared at Lonnie. "Lonnie, do we have anymore bleach in the back?"

"Yeah," he answered, focused entirely on his magazine.

She jumped up and placed her hand on her hip. She approached him. "It's an hour till closing. Are you planning on doing anything to clean up for tomorrow?"

He closed his magazine, "It don't take an hour to shut this place down."

She sighed, "Maybe some of us want to leave at ten on the dot!"

"I don't know why. Clyde ain't coming to pick your ass up. Why you think he dropped his little rug rats here on you anyway?" he grinned. "He's out kicking it with his lady. Candy's probably wearing your old man out."

She rolled her eyes, "You said the bleach is in the back, right?"

He chuckled, "Yeah, right where we keep the mops and the brooms."

She angrily marched to the back of the store. His eyes followed her hips all the way off of the front line. He promptly turned his attention to the kids in the dining room. The boys had both bowed their heads on the table falling slowly asleep. He turned the music in the dining room up a notch and calmly strolled to the back of the store.

Brenda was in the back, bent over searching through the stock closet. Lonnie walked up and stood directly behind her. He smiled as he was amused by her position.

"Where is it?" she muttered to herself.

"It's in there!" said Lonnie.

Frightened, she quickly jumped up and turned around, "I thought I asked you to quit walking up on me like that!"

"Ain't nobody walked up on you," he replied. "This is walking up on you." He stepped closer. They were almost touching toes.

"Lonnie," she paused, "I don't know what the hell is wrong with you, but I'm about to leave right now! I warned you already." She leaned away from him.

He grabbed her arm, "You ain't going no where! We're talking."

She stared at his hand, almost shocked, "Lonnie! Get your hands off me, fool."

"Hell nah!" he said as he swung her into the wall.

"Lonnie!" she cried.

He quickly covered her mouth with his hand and aggressively pressed his body against hers. "You've been trotting around here for too long not to be giving me any," he laughed as he took his other hand and began unzipping his pants. "I know how you like it. You like it how Clyde gives it to you, but I can give it to you much better, baby!"

She tried valiantly to scream, but his hand was pressed too tightly against her mouth.

"You like it rough, baby, I know."

He unbuckled his pants and they slid onto the floor. He quickly began to unbutton her shirt. Her eyes began to bulge out of her head.

"I'm gonna give it to you nice and rough," he said as he unzipped her pants.

As a last resort, she bit down on his pinky finger.

"Ah shit!" he screamed.

He quickly covered his hand. She pushed him aside and kicked him in his family jewels. He fell to the floor like a sack of potatoes. "Goddamn it!" he screamed. "You little bitch!"

She nervously stared at him for a moment while she zipped her pants up. She turned her attention to the front line and began to run. He quickly grabbed her by her leg, propelling her onto the floor. The fall knocked all of the wind out of her. In pain, she grabbed her belly.

Lonnie managed to get up on his knees and crawled to her. "You stupid ho! I wasn't even gonna be that rough!"

He rolled her over and slapped her on her face. She instantly bled from the corner of her mouth.

He grabbed his crouch, "You know you want this." He crawled on top of her. "Don't you want this? Don't you?"

"Yeah," she screamed.

With all of her muscle, she kneed him in his private parts again.

"Shit!" he screamed as he rolled over on the floor, grabbing his crouch.

She rapidly backed away from him as he rolled over on the floor in pain.

"Brenda!" Deshawn screamed out of the dining room.

With her mouth wide open, she looked towards the front. She hopped to her feet and limped onto the front line. She hastily stopped in her tracks as she stood face to face with a man hiding his face underneath a black mask, pointing a gun at her.

"Oh, God, it's the robber!" she screamed. She looked towards the dining room and noticed the boys lying on the floor with their hands over their heads.

"Hey you-- don't make a move!" yelled the masked man.

She struggled to catch her breath as she raised both of her hands.

"Where's the manager?" screamed the man.

"He's in the back," she nervously yelled, "He's in the back."

Lonnie ran behind Brenda with his pants hanging off of his butt. He paused at the sight of the gunman. "Son of a bitch!" he screamed.

"Alright, don't move!" yelled the gunman as he angled his gun towards Lonnie's face. He frowned, "What the hell were you two doing back there, anyway?"

"Nothing," replied Lonnie.

"Yeah, I bet," said the robber as he approached the two. "Lead me to the safe!"

The masked man grabbed Brenda's wrist and pushed Lonnie forward, directing him to the back of the store. Lonnie guided them to the office. Brenda nervously stared at the robber, in awe of the whole situation.

"Open the safe and do it fast!" demanded the masked man.

Lonnie quickly fell to his knees and began turning the combination on the lock as the gunman kept his gun pointed against the back of his neck. The masked man turned to Brenda and observed her.

"You alright?" asked the gunman.

She frowned, "How do you expect me to feel?"

"Hey, just asking! You look like you've been in a cat-fight or something!"

"You'd look this way, too, if your manager just tried to rape you!"

"Oh he did!" said the gunman.

"That's a goddamn lie!" yelled Lonnie as he paused and glanced back at Brenda.

The masked man violently smashed Lonnie on the side of his forehead with the pistol, "Didn't I tell you to open that freakin' safe, you pervert?"

Lonnie rubbed the side of his head that had began to bleed profusely, "Alright, Alright!" he uttered as he began turning the safe's combination again.

The gunman released Brenda's wrist and turned his back to her, focusing completely on Lonnie. She gazed at the man, almost surprised he let his guard down to her. She thought she somehow knew this masked man. Why did he even care about how she looked? Or if she was alright? He was suppose to be the bad guy, right?

"You're taking too long. You better hurry up!" yelled the gunman. He kicked Lonnie in his butt. "You fat jerk! You ought to be ashamed of yourself, trying to rape a woman. Wasn't your mother a woman?"

She backed out of the office as she thought his voice sounded somewhat familiar. He continued to ramble on about what Lonnie had tried to do, as if it had upset him. Who was this masked man that she didn't know, that obviously knew her, who had some kind of feelings towards her?

Finally, Lonnie managed to open the safe. "It's open," he announced. He frantically backed away as the gunman leaned over him and briefly glanced into the dark safe.

"Okay, just give me all the deposits. You can keep the change!"

Lonnie anxiously handed the man three deposit bags.

"Thank you," said the gunman.

He kneed Lonnie in his face, driving him onto the floor. The man turned around and stared at Brenda, who was frozen in her tracks. He stuffed the deposits in his pockets.

"I suggest you get out of here shortly after I leave," replied the gunman. "That guy is more of a criminal than I am." He swiftly ran onto the front line of the store.

"Wait!" she screamed as she followed him.

The man stopped right before he reached the door. "Lady, it's not safe to chase a man that's just got finished robbing you," he said as he turned around.

She slowly approached him, somewhat uncertain about what she was doing. "I know you, don't I?"

"Look, let me leave, okay?"

"I'm not twisting your arm to stay. You stopped because you wanted to. You know me, and I surely know you!" She stood face to face with the masked man.

"Lady, don't make me hurt you!" he said as he turned around and pushed the door open.

"Wait!" she yelled. "Take me with you!"

"What?" he asked as he faced her.

"I want to go with you..." she said as she pulled up his mask.

"...Miguel!"

It was Miguel! He stood frozen as they calmly stared into each other's eyes.

"Somehow I knew it was you all along," she grinned as a tear slid down her face. "I wanted it to be you."

He finished pulling the mask off of his head. "I didn't expect you to be here tonight. If I knew I wouldn't have..." He bowed his head. "I've been casing this spot for weeks."

She blushed, "I guess it was my destiny to be here tonight!"

They giggled. He leaned down a gave her a soft kiss. He pulled away.

"Take me with you, Miguel," she demanded.

"You don't..."

"Yes, I wanna be with you," she cried, "I don't care where you're going. I don't have to know where it's going to lead. I just want to be there with you to experience it."

He blushed as he tightly hugged her. Suddenly, gunshots sprang out. It was Lonnie, firing his pistol like he was a madman.

"I knew you were hiding something, Romeo!" he screamed while firing shots at Miguel.

Miguel pushed Brenda aside and blasted Lonnie on the side of his leg with his pistol. Lonnie dropped his gun and fell backwards onto the floor. The back of his head collided with the wall, knocking him unconscious. The children in the dining room screamed. Miguel ran to Lonnie's body, placing his hand beside his neck to check his pulse.

"Is he alive?" asked Brenda.

"He'll make it, but his head is gonna hurt like hell when he wakes up." Miguel stood up and kicked Lonnie's gun aside. He walked to Brenda and held out his hand, "Are you sure you want to be a part of this movie?"

She smiled, "Only if it has an happy ending."

Miguel blushed, "Oh, I'm working on it!" He grabbed her hand. "Come on!"

They ran off of the front line and headed towards the exit.

Travon jumped off of the floor and stood up straight with his hands on his waist, "Hey, where do you think you're going?"

Brenda smirked, "Somewhere far, far away from you and your no-good daddy!"

"I'ma tell daddy!" he yelled.

"Tell him!" she laughed.

Hand and hand, she ran out of the restaurant by Miguel's side. They jumped into a late model BMW convertible, gave each other a kiss and rolled out of the Chicken Coop's parking lot.

The End